Praise for Cynthia Kadohata
A Million Shades of Gray

★ "Kadohata delves deep into the soul of her protagonist while making a faraway place and the stark consequences of war seem very near. Y'Tin's inner conflicts and changing perception of the world will haunt readers." —*Publishers Weekly*, starred review

"Kadohata depicts the questions, fears, confusion, and apprehension skillfully. Y'Tin is a thoughtful young man searching for clear answers where there are none." —*School Library Journal*

"This remarkable work of historic fiction powerfully evokes a specific time and place while exploring issues pertinent to any war." —*The Washington Post*

A Million Shades of Gray

CYNTHIA KADOHATA

A Million Shades of Gray

Atheneum Books for Young Readers
New York London Toronto Sydney New Delhi

To Sammy,
light of my life

ATHENEUM BOOKS FOR YOUNG READERS
An imprint of Simon & Schuster Children's Publishing Division
1230 Avenue of the Americas, New York, New York 10020

ATHENEUM BOOKS FOR YOUNG READERS
is a registered trademark of Simon & Schuster, Inc.
For information about special discounts for bulk purchases, please contact
Simon & Schuster Special Sales at 1-866-506-1949 or business@simonandschuster.com.
The Simon & Schuster Speakers Bureau can bring authors to your live event.
For more information or to book an event, contact the Simon & Schuster Speakers Bureau
at 1-866-248-3049 or visit our website at www.simonspeakers.com.
Also available in an Atheneum Books for Young Readers hardcover edition
Book design by Mike Rosamilia
The text for this book is set in Berkeley Oldstyle Book.
Manufactured in the United States of America
1213 OPM
First Atheneum Books for Young Readers paperback edition November 2011
4 6 8 10 9 7 5 3
The Library of Congress has cataloged the hardcover edition as follows:
Kadohata, Cynthia.
A million shades of gray / Cynthia Kadohata.—1st ed
p.   cm.
Summary: In 1975 after American troops pull out of Vietnam, a thirteen-year-old boy and
his beloved elephant escape into the jungle when the Viet Cong attack his village.
ISBN 978-1-4169-1883-7 (hc)
1. Vietnam—History—1975—Juvenile fiction. [1. Vietnam—History—1975—Fiction.
2. Elephants—Fiction. 3. Survival—Fiction.] I. Title.
PZ7.K1166Mi 2010
[Fic]—dc22   2009033307
ISBN 978-1-4424-2919-2 (pbk)
ISBN 978-1-4169-9859-4 (eBook)

Chapter One

1973, Central Highlands, South Vietnam

Y'Tin Eban watched Tomas fasten the rope around Lady's neck. Lady was the smallest of the village's three elephants, but she was also the strongest, so she was much in demand as a worker. Today Lady would be dragging logs for the Buonya clan. The Buonyas' house had caught fire and they were building a new one.

Y'Tin stood just in back and to the side of Tomas. Sometimes Tomas got annoyed at how closely Y'Tin stood, but Y'Tin didn't want to miss anything. On the other hand, Y'Tin didn't want to annoy Tomas too much or he might refuse to train Y'Tin further. At fourteen Tomas Knul was the youngest elephant handler ever in the village, but

Y'Tin hoped to beat that record. Y'Tin was only eleven, but he was confident that he would be a fine elephant handler someday.

"Stand back," Tomas snapped. "Or I won't let you work with the elephants today."

Y'Tin dutifully stepped back. He did whatever Tomas told him to do. There were other kids who hung around the elephants, but Y'Tin was the one Tomas had chosen to train. Tomas had assured him that when the time was right, Y'Tin would become Lady's handler. Y'Tin didn't want him to change his mind.

One of the kids who hung around got too close, and Y'Tin snapped, "Stand back," just as Tomas had snapped to him.

Tomas glanced at Y'Tin. "I was thinking I'd let you ride her into the village today. I'll walk beside you. Do you think you're ready?"

"I'm ready," Y'Tin said. He had been ready for months. He patted Lady's side; she ignored him.

Tomas looked at him thoughtfully. "I think you want to be an elephant handler even more than I once did."

"Sure thing," Y'Tin said in English. He had learned that from one of the American Special

2

Forces soldiers his father knew. The Americans had many words for "yes." "Sure," "okay," "right," "affirmative," "absolutely," "yeah," "check," "Roger that," and "sure do, tennis shoe" came immediately to mind.

Y'Tin walked around to Lady's trunk to have a talk with her. "I'm going to ride you in today, Lady. You need to behave yourself."

As if in answer, Lady pushed him to the ground with her trunk. And she didn't let him up. It was embarrassing. He tried to get away, but Lady was too strong. "Tomas," he said. "Uh, can you help me?"

Tomas rolled his eyes. "Lady!" he said sharply, and Lady let Y'Tin up. "You've got to be firmer with her," Tomas scolded Y'Tin. "Use your hook to keep her in line."

"But I want her to like me."

"You want her to respect you. Now help get those logs attached to her rope." Y'Tin and one of the Buonya boys tied logs to the end of the rope attached to Lady's harness. She would haul the logs to the building site.

When the logs were secure, Y'Tin said, "*Muk,* Lady." But she refused to kneel. "*Muk!*" He noticed

Tomas looking at him. *"Muk!"* he said again. Y'Tin could feel his face growing hot. He took his stick with the hook and poked her with it. She still didn't respond.

"Lady, *muk*," Tomas said mildly, and she immediately knelt.

Y'Tin climbed aboard her, his legs straddling her back. "Lady, up," Y'Tin said, and for once she listened.

"Lady, *nao*," Tomas said, and she calmly followed him, dragging the three huge logs behind her.

Y'Tin felt a rush of happiness. When they reached the gate to the village, he sat up with his chest sticking out proudly. Lady followed Tomas to the site where the new longhouse would be built. The Buonyas were one of the biggest clans in the village, so they were planning a house one hundred meters long. That translated to a lot of logs.

And so it went for the rest of the afternoon, with Lady and Y'Tin going back and forth from the jungle to the site. At one point Lady actually knelt when he told her to. It was just about the best day of Y'Tin's life.

That night as he lay in his family's room in the

clan's longhouse, the others slept while he stayed up going over and over the whole afternoon. He could see Lady clearly when he closed his eyes. He felt giddy. Everyone kept saying that he was too young to know what his future held, but he knew as well as he knew anything that he would spend his life as an elephant handler. Still, his father had told him to always think about "the other hand." So, on the other hand, he had been working with Lady for many months now and he didn't seem to be making much headway with her. Today when she knelt and stood up on command were the first times she had ever listened to him.

Tomas always warned him not to become too friendly with her or she wouldn't respect him. He liked to remind Y'Tin of the time a few years ago when Lady went into a rage for some mysterious reason. Y'Tin still remembered the huge gap in the fence that she had stampeded.

Y'Tin's father was sleeping fitfully, mumbling about the Americans. His father had a lot on his mind lately. He worked with the American Special Forces and had been talking to Y'Tin's mother about the possibility of becoming a Christian. He hadn't made any decisions about it yet. He often

5

took a long time to make a decision. For instance, it had taken him nearly two years to allow Y'Tin to work with the elephants, and it had taken him a year to decide to work with the Americans.

So far the remoteness of the village had saved it from the worst of what the Americans called the Vietnam War and what his father called the American War. Y'Tin hoped the war would be over by the time he was grown. North and South Vietnam had been fighting since well before Y'Tin was born. The Americans fought with the South.

All his father thought about was the war, and all Y'Tin thought about was elephants. Y'Tin knew he was different from the other boys in that he did not want to be a farmer. That's why his parents worried about him so much. There was just one thing that he wanted: to be an elephant handler. Meanwhile, Y'Tin did so poorly in school that his parents were disappointed in him. His older sister, H'Juaih, got highest marks. He was proud of her, but that didn't mean he wanted to be like her.

"Y'Tin?" his mother called out from the darkness.

"Yes, Ami."

"I knew you were still awake."

And, indeed, she often did know when he was awake, though he didn't make a sound. He never knew whether she was awake or sleeping. Either way, she was silent.

"Are you daydreaming again?"

He didn't answer.

"If you spent as much time on your homework as you do on your daydreaming, your grades would be the same as H'Juaih's."

"Ami, I was just thinking. That's different from daydreaming."

"How is it different?" his mother responded.

"Daydreaming is thinking about things that aren't true yet. Thinking is when you ponder matters that are already true."

She didn't answer, and he knew he had won the argument. On the other hand, maybe she just stopped talking because she was tired. He was tired also. He closed his eyes and watched Lady until he fell asleep.

7

Chapter Two

B efore sunup, Y'Tin woke to hear his mother shaking his father awake. "Sergeant Shepard wants to talk to you," she told him in a low voice.

"What?" Ama said sleepily. Y'Tin heard his father rustling, probably sitting up.

"Sergeant Shepard," his mother repeated.

Y'Tin sat up too. "Are you going on a mission, Ama?" he asked.

"I don't know," his father said. "I'll find out from Shepard. You go back to sleep."

Instead, Y'Tin stood up. "Can I come if you go on a mission? Remember when you told me someday I could?"

"I said someday *maybe* you could."

"Ama, I could track for you. You know I'm a good tracker."

"I know. Go back to sleep," Ama said.

"Go to sleep, Y'Tin," Ami said.

Y'Tin waited until his father had slipped out of the room and then he followed. At the front porch Y'Tin stood just inside the door watching. Shepard nodded at him and he nodded back. A cigarette hung from Shepard's mouth, as usual. Y'Tin's heart speeded up, but not in a bad way. The Americans had announced that they would be leaving Vietnam soon, and this might be Y'Tin's last chance to go on a mission with his father.

"You got cigarette for me?" Y'Tin's father asked Shepard in English.

Shepard handed him a cigarette. Y'Tin knew his father thought the cigarettes that his tribe rolled themselves tasted better than the American cigarettes, yet for some reason he enjoyed smoking the American cigarettes more.

His father said "Ahhhh" when he exhaled. He

always did that when he started his first cigarette of the day.

"I get cigarette too?" Y'Tin asked in English.

"Your mother told me you don't smoke," Shepard said. "She said you're just a little boy."

Y'Tin laughed. "I old for my age."

"How do you figure?"

"Got too many responsibilities. Very stressful."

"Go on inside, Y'Tin," his father said. "Go on, boy." But he didn't say it angrily or even very seriously. If he had, Y'Tin would have gone back inside.

The men climbed down the notched log that served as a ladder for the longhouse. Y'Tin followed. A couple more Special Forces soldiers were standing just a few meters away with two Rhade tribal members. Shepard, Y'Tin's father, and Y'Tin joined them. Shepard squatted and put his cigarette out on the ground, then put the filter in a bag in his pocket. This way, he wouldn't leave a mess on the Rhade ground. The Americans were very considerate.

Shepard turned to Y'Tin's father. "We got one last thing we need done. Y'Thu, we need you to be our tracker to a former enemy camp. We know loosely where there was a North Vietnamese Army company last week, and we need to see how many soldiers were there. We're not expecting any contact with the enemy. It's just a few klicks away, but it's slow going. Very heavy jungle. You available to spend the night in the field?"

Y'Tin's father blushed. "I got to talk to my wife first," he mumbled. "She thought I all finish with this stuff." Y'Tin knew that since the Americans were leaving in a couple of weeks, his father had been told that he wouldn't be needed for any more missions.

"I understand. Go on and talk to your wife. Make sure to tell her this mission is supposed to be smooth sailing."

"What 'smooth sailing' mean?" asked Y'Tin. "Easy mission?" Y'Tin turned to his father and spoke in Rhade. "Ama, you ask Ami if I can come too? I promise I'll do my homework for a week."

"Why not do your homework forever?" his father asked.

"Forever," Y'Tin said solemnly, but his father just laughed at him.

His father jogged over to their longhouse and climbed up. His mother was already on the porch, watching them.

Y'Tin turned to Shepard. "It bad luck to go now. You tempting the spirits."

"Just this last mission. It's no contact with the enemy," Shepard assured him.

"I come too?"

"Let's see what your mother and father say."

Y'Tin's father climbed down again. "Okay?" Shepard asked.

"Okay," Y'Tin's father said. "You let my son come?"

"Yep, if you want. It's smooth sailing."

Y'Tin's heart fluttered. Riding Lady into the village and now this. What a week!

"All right, we need to get a move on," Shepard said.

Y'Tin didn't know what a "move on" was and where they might get one, but he didn't ask.

Shepard continued. "We got the order an hour ago. We need you—you *and* your son—to find the camp and estimate how many were there. I don't know what for, the powers that be just requested the information. And who's the best tracker I've ever worked with?"

"Ah," Y'Tin's father said, feigning modesty. Then he seemed to ponder for a moment before saying less modestly, "I guess I pretty good, if I say so myself."

"We took the liberty of packing for you. Canteen, PIR rations, ammunition. And here's your rifle."

"What I need rifle for?"

"Nothing, but if we do need them, we should have them."

"Gotcha, G.I."

"Okay, let's get started. Remember, no contact. You see anything suspicious, you let us know, and we'll back off. Nobody wants to get hurt this late in the game."

"Gotcha, G.I."

Ama patted Y'Tin's shoulder proudly. Then he looked worried. "We make sacrifice first? My wife suggested."

"The sun is starting to come up. It's getting late," Shepard said.

"Don't say I no warn you."

"We won't."

They all entered the jungle together. Y'Tin's senses seemed so alive, he felt almost inhuman. Everyone said he was part elephant, and maybe that was true.

Y'Tin walked by his father's side. He felt very

proud. And he really loved to feel very proud. And he loved walking in front of the other men.

He put his whole being into tracking, just as if he were stalking prey. He walked so quietly that he couldn't hear himself, and that made him feel proud as well. They moved very slowly for several kilometers. Then Y'Tin saw them: several tracks, crossing their pathway. He noticed before his father did. He dropped to his hands and knees and studied the tracks. Six different soldiers. They made six distinct prints: One walked with his toes pointed slightly in; another had small feet—possibly a woman; one left different tread marks from the others; one came down hard on the heels; another had the second smallest feet; and one made a telltale scuff as he lifted his feet. Y'Tin's father squatted down beside him and then nodded in encouragement. "Six soldiers," Y'Tin said. He stood up and his father followed suit. Then Y'Tin saw the pride in his father's face as he looked at Y'Tin.

As they followed the tracks, there were times when Y'Tin almost lost the trail. The others kept waiting for him silently—he always took a little longer than his father to figure out what the tracks were telling him. His father had once told him that every trail told a story and the important thing was not to read the story the fastest but, rather, the most accurately. Y'Tin knew that Ama could read faster *and* more accurately than he could.

The six soldiers had sanitized their tracks very well. But you could never sanitize your trail completely. A broken twig, a bent blade of grass—there would always be a sign of where you were going, of where you'd been. Y'Tin glanced back at Shepard and at Ama's friend Y'Bier Hlong, who was sanitizing *their* trail. With about 100,000 members, the Rhade—Y'Tin's tribe—was one of the biggest Dega tribes in Vietnam, and many of the Rhade worked with the American Special Forces. In Y'Tin's village, however, there were only a few men who worked with the Americans. Who knew why?

The trail disappeared, but Y'Tin and his father continued in the same direction as before. After about forty meters they picked up the trail again. Y'Tin's father gestured with his hand, and they turned right, just as the trail did.

Twenty minutes later the trail split in two. Y'Tin studied the split and noticed that nobody had even stopped to talk: One trail of five prints simply went to the right, and the other trail—of just one soldier—

went left. He thought about that, knelt, and studied the fork. He looked at his father. One way or another, his father had to make a call. Ama opted to follow the trail of five over the trail of one. That's what Y'Tin would have chosen as well.

After about an hour Y'Tin realized they'd made a mistake when he saw the trail of five men heading out of the jungle. His father always said you had to tell the truth when you made a mistake, because in life when you told one lie, that always led to two lies, and the two lies led to four, until your whole life became a lie. Y'Tin thought that was an exaggeration, but he got the point.

Ama turned to the men and held himself proudly as he gestured with his hand that they were turning around.

When they reached the fork again, they followed the tracks of the one soldier this time. His trail led deep into the jungle. It was late afternoon when they reached the end of the trail. There was no debris left, but this was where the enemy had gathered. The area was full of disturbed vegetation and dirt. Y'Tin stepped in a patch of undisturbed ground and compared it to the footprints he was examining. His fresh print slowly recovered, but some of the succulent plants he'd stepped on were permanently broken. Ama signaled the others to stop as he circled the site and slipped in and out of the abandoned camp. Y'Tin saw that his father was counting every print, but Y'Tin used the averaging method. He split the camp into quarters and counted the number of people in one quarter. It took Y'Tin three hours to count and feel sure he was close to correct. He tried not to feel the pressure, but he wished he could work faster. It was growing dark by the time he finished. His father had finished a half hour earlier, but everybody waited for Y'Tin. Finally, he turned to his father and said, "About one hundred fifty."

His father nodded. "That's what I came up with. One hundred twenty-five to one hundred fifty."

Suddenly, and clearly, they heard talking, and the whole group—seven of them in all—melted into the forest. That is, Y'Tin knew the others melted into the forest, as he did. The only one he could see was Shepard. Then whoever had been talking fell silent. Y'Tin could just barely hear the other men gingerly walking backward. He wondered whether the Special Forces soldiers would open fire, but they didn't. None of his group moved for a full hour. Then all hell broke loose. Shooting exploded behind Y'Tin, before him, and above him. His group was doing some of the shooting. Then Y'Bier Hlong staggered into sight. His chest gushed blood as he dropped his rifle. Y'Tin picked it up. He'd never shot a gun. He pointed it toward an enemy soldier but hesitated—he wasn't sure where everybody was and didn't want to accidentally hit one of the friendlies. Then a North Vietnamese soldier was aiming at Shepard's back, and Y'Tin fired. The bullet shot upward, and the backfire was so strong that Y'Tin fell to the ground. By the time he scrambled up, the firefight had ended. Shepard was taking Y'Bier's pulse. Fortunately, someone else must have shot the soldier who'd been aiming at Shepard.

Silence. Shepard hung his head, and Y'Tin knew that his father's friend had died, shot in the chest and head. Y'Tin stared at him. He had never seen someone killed before.

They walked until it was pitch dark, with Shepard carrying Y'Bier. After a while Shepard said one word: "Here." The men lay on the ground for sleep. Y'Tin stared into the darkness. Soon he heard a soft, soft sound and realized it was his father crying. Y'Tin fell asleep to the sound. He woke up just once, his face clammy with dew, and he still heard the sound. Ama had worked for the Special Forces for several years, but he'd been lucky—this was the first time anyone had been killed on one of his father's missions. Y'Tin knew it was his fault. If they hadn't waited for him to finish counting, Y'Bier never would have been shot. Was the guilt he felt part of war? He could feel that Y'Bier's three souls had already left the body. Y'Bier was the nicest man in the village. He always gave away all of the delicious cantaloupes that he raised every year. Y'Tin's family grew the best tobacco, but they didn't give it away like that. No one did, just the Hlongs.

The next morning Shepard carried the dead man on his back all the way to the village. He gently laid Y'Bier in the graveyard just outside the fence.

"Get a blanket, Y'Tin," his father told him.

Y'Tin half flew to his longhouse and scrambled up. Nobody was there—they were all no doubt working in the fields. He ran back to the cemetery to lay the blanket over Y'Bier's body. But he saw he was too late. Somehow, Y'Bier's wife had already heard and was weeping over the bloody body.

Y'Tin wanted to tell her that it was all his fault, but instead, he just stared at her.

Chapter Three

1975

Y'Tin scrubbed Lady's hide as hard as he could. She lay on her side in the river, filling her trunk with water and spraying it on herself and, sometimes, on him. He suspected she sprayed him on purpose, but he couldn't be sure. Either way, his shirt and loincloth were drenched.

"Now I'll be all wet for school!" he exclaimed. Then he laughed and slapped her side—what he always did when he had finished washing her. She stood up and filled her trunk with mud, which she blew onto her back. Elephants' bodies made much more heat than human beings' bodies, and they kept cooler by covering their backs with mud. Y'Tin had learned that years ago, when he first became obsessed with elephants.

The other elephant keepers had already finished washing their elephants. Y'Tin always took longest because he was a perfectionist. Anyway, that's why he thought he took longest. "Lady, *nao!*" he said. She started down the path to her pen. Her spongy feet fell silently on the jungle floor. Even when she stepped on a twig, the noise was muffled by her feet. Someday, after the war ended, he might go to school to study elephants. Or maybe he would start his own elephant-training school.

Lady stopped to pull at some tree bark. Y'Tin said, *"Nao!"* and she lowered her trunk and continued silently down the path. He was one of the only elephant keepers he'd ever heard of who didn't use a stick with a hook at the end to communicate with his elephant. That was one of the skills he would teach if he ever opened an elephant-training school. He had heard there were such schools in Thailand, but he'd never heard of such a thing in Vietnam. His would be the first. He had become the youngest elephant keeper ever, and he would open the first elephant school in Vietnam. Who knew what other records he might break?

Two years ago, when he'd become the youngest elephant keeper—ever!—he had used the hook, because otherwise, Lady wouldn't listen to him. But as they had grown familiar with each other, he used the hook less and less until he finally abandoned it altogether. He did carry it with him, just in case he needed it in some sort of emergency, but he hadn't used it for about a year.

Y'Tin had just broken into a jog to keep up with Lady when she stopped walking and knocked him to the ground with her trunk. He couldn't help laughing. He got up, and she knocked him down again. It was her favorite game, but he knew she would stop if he told her to. He held her trunk a second and scratched it. When he let go, she let it sway softly one way and then another. *"Muk,"* he said, and she knelt. He climbed over her head and sat just past her shoulders, in front of where the mud was already caking. He rubbed her neck, pushing down her bristly hairs. She shook her head *no*.

"What is it?" he asked.

She shook her head again, and he felt her mood change. Maybe she sensed the tiger that had been haunting the village. His sisters had seen the

tiger yesterday. Y'Tin looked around but saw nothing except jungle. Then he heard men speaking
Vietnamese instead of Rhade. "I'm telling you, the
river is that way," one said.

Two South Vietnamese soldiers stepped onto
the path right in front of Lady. Even though South
Vietnam and the Dega had both fought on the
American side of the war, soldiers frightened him.

"*Moi!*" one said to Y'Tin. "*Moi!*" *Moi* meant "sav-
age." It was what the Vietnamese—both North and
South—called Y'Tin's people. But no one had ever
personally called Y'Tin a *moi*. He felt anger rise in
his chest, but he remained silent. The soldiers carried guns, and you never knew what might happen
with men carrying guns. The soldiers might shoot
him dead right there and not think of it ever again.
That was what war did to people. His father had said
so. And if his father said it, it was the truth. Y'Tin
waited to see what the soldiers would do next.

"Where's the river?" the taller of the two men
demanded.

Y'Tin pointed behind him.

The man seemed to be cleaning his teeth with
his tongue for several seconds. Then he scratched
at a tooth with a finger before returning his

attention to Y'Tin. "Don't you know how to talk?" he finally said.

"You follow the path," Y'Tin said in Vietnamese. He bowed his head subserviently a couple of times, for he could see they were in a bad mood. They stood before him for a moment longer, and he wondered what was coming next. Then the tall one said, "Let's go" to the other, and they left.

Y'Tin felt Lady relax as she continued down the path. "Who are they to call me *moi*, eh, Lady?" He slapped the side of her neck. They emerged from the jungle near the elephant pen that Y'Tin and the other keepers had built several years ago, before Y'Tin was officially an elephant keeper. They had wanted to make sure a roof covered the elephants during sunny days. Even with mud caked on their backs, the elephants still liked to relax in the pen. Y'Tin had also built a small hutch for himself, so he could sleep near Lady every night. Originally, he had wanted to build his own longhouse. He had liked to mention to people how he was going to be the youngest handler ever, even though he'd already told everyone. In fact, one day he had said to his father, "Ama, since I'm going to be the youngest elephant keeper someday, maybe I should have

24

my own longhouse by the elephant pen."

His father had replied, "If you build it, you can have it."

"I can't build it on my own. I was thinking that since I'm going to be the youngest elephant keeper ever, you would help me."

His father had laughed. "When I was hunting at your age, nobody built me a longhouse."

So Y'Tin didn't get his own longhouse. All he could build by himself was the hutch.

Now Y'Tin looked toward his family's land and saw his mother and father weeding in their tobacco field. Sometimes people commented that his father loved tobacco as much as Y'Tin loved elephants.

Every day the villagers worked in their fields as if there were no war raging. The last American soldiers had left Vietnam in 1973, and after that daily life continued. Y'Tin's father still worked in his beloved tobacco field, and Y'Tin still went to school, still took care of Lady. He fantasized that the North Vietnamese Army and the Vietcong would leave them alone and that his people would remain in the Central Highlands, where they had lived for hundreds—maybe thousands—of years.

The tribes' other two elephants, Geng and Dok,

were already chained and waiting patiently until their elephant keepers finished working in the fields. Geng was the Knuls' elephant and was handled by Tomas, and Dok belonged to the Hwings and was handled by a boy named Y'Siu.

The chains were long enough to allow the elephants to reach the bamboo trees and tall grass in the jungle but too short to allow them to reach the fields owned by Y'Tin's family. Y'Tin wasn't supposed to, but in July when the sugarcane was ripe, he cut plenty of canes for Lady. It was her favorite thing. He always cut off the sweet end for Lady and gave the rest to Geng and Dok. He knew Lady was more spoiled than the others, but she was also the hardest working. Still, sometimes Tomas reprimanded Y'Tin for spoiling Lady. At sixteen Tomas was the oldest, so Y'Tin and Y'Siu always deferred to him. One day Y'Tin had suggested they chain the elephants farther out because there was a bigger bamboo stand there. Tomas had pursed his lips and said, "They're fine where they are." Y'Tin was a little miffed, but Tomas was the boss man.

Besides a few minor run-ins with Tomas, the only difficult time Y'Tin had experienced as an elephant keeper was before he began training. A man from another village had wanted to breed his bull with Lady. She'd gotten pregnant and, at twenty-two months, had given birth to a male, whom Y'Tin had named Mountain. That was when he built a little house, so he could give round-the-clock attention to Lady and Mountain. But Mountain had died at six months, and Lady had been depressed for a long time. She lost so much weight that her ribs stuck out. Y'Tin lost weight as well, until his own ribs stuck out. That was something Y'Tin and Lady had gone through together, and after that they had been connected by their spirits.

Now Lady was pregnant again by a wild bull who'd stormed the village. That was twenty-one months ago, meaning Lady might give birth at any time. For reasons not understood, nobody in the village had ever successfully raised a calf of a domesticated elephant, but Y'Tin planned to be the first.

Now he attached Lady's chain to her leg and gave her trunk a good scratch. "I'll see you after school," he told her, but her attention had already turned to a bamboo tree. It was ridiculous, but even before he left, he was already feeling lonely for her. Y'Tin was the last elephant handler back from the river, as he was every morning. While he attended school, Lady would stay chained here unless there was work for her to do hauling wood or crops.

Y'Tin walked toward the village. The fence surrounding it was made of bamboo stalks sharpened at the tops. Years ago the Americans had wanted many villages to put up fences. The fences were to protect the village as well as to let the Vietcong know that this village did not support them. Y'Tin walked through the gate, on which hung the green, red, and white flag of his people. A drawing of an elephant decorated the flag, so naturally, Y'Tin approved of it.

He moved quickly past the longhouses, which all looked the same: slanting thatch roofs and stilts several feet high holding up the structures. The houses were built north to south. He had heard that in America nearly every house looked different from the house next to it and houses could face different directions, depending on how the street ran. Y'Tin thought that seemed disorganized, but who was he to judge?

As he approached his family's longhouse, he clucked at the chicken coop and opened the door.

The chickens scurried out to forage. They were a motley collection: red, black, white, brown. Once, a Special Forces soldier had watched with interest as Y'Tin clucked for the chickens in the evening. He'd asked Y'Tin how he knew which chickens were his and not another villager's. Y'Tin tried to be polite but laughed a bit when he explained, "We know which chickens are ours, and they know us." Sometimes the Americans were funny. He really missed them. And they had a lot of weapons to fight the North Vietnamese and the Vietcong. In the Central Highlands, life had seemed safer when the Americans had been here, even though Y'Tin had heard gunfire almost every night. He still heard gunfire.

Y'Tin climbed the ladder up to his longhouse. At 130 meters long, it was the biggest in the village. His entire clan numbered sixty, not counting the two babies who were still in their mothers' stomachs. Y'Tin had never set foot in parts of his house. He mostly just went from the entrance to his family's room. One of his aunties lived at the far end, in the biggest room. She was a widow and had her room all to herself. Though she was just thirty-two, she had been widowed three times, and, frankly, after that nobody was too keen on marrying her.

Y'Tin nodded to one of his seven uncles, who sat on a mat eating rice in the entrance room. His uncle chewed and swallowed.

"Do a good job in school today," his uncle said. "You know how important it is to your mother."

"I'll study hard," Y'Tin said, but he knew his uncle didn't believe him. Nobody ever believed him when he said that. Maybe he should start saying something new when people told him to do a good job in school. Maybe he should say *Absolutely*, the way the Americans would have.

Y'Tin went to the family bedroom to grab his schoolbook. He looked at it with distaste. Most days he couldn't even bear to open it up. One thing about school was that even though all the children were different, they all used the same book. Did that make sense?

He didn't feel he should have to attend school. As an elephant expert, he would always have work. The village would always need elephants. He begged his parents again and again to let him stay home. He would work on them for a few weeks and then not say anything for another few weeks, so that each time he complained, it would seem fresh to them. He thought he might be wearing them down, because sometimes after he begged them, he saw his parents meet eyes in a certain way, the way they did when they disagreed but didn't want to say so in front of Y'Tin and his sisters.

School was really his mother's idea, and his father always supported her when it came to raising Y'Tin, H'Juaih, and his younger sister, nicknamed Jujubee. Rhade women could be bossy. Y'Tin had heard that the women were more subservient in some of the other thirty-odd Dega tribes here in the Central Highlands. But in the Rhade tribe the women held a lot of power. His mother wanted him to go to school so that he could move to the city one day. "That way, you can have a better life," she liked to say. He tried to explain to her that he didn't want a better life. Except for school, his life was fine the way it was. Maybe after Lady died he would check out the city. But Lady was just twenty-one, and elephants lived to sixty or even longer. In forty years Y'Tin would be fifty-three. Then, and only then, he might want this better life his mother spoke of. But he didn't like to think of

Lady dying. Sometimes, even though her death was many years away, he cried when he thought of her dying.

Nobody else was around except his uncle. His sisters had no doubt left for school quite a while ago, and the rest of the clan was working in the fields. Y'Tin glanced at them as he left the village. Every day was nearly the same for them. But every day was different for Y'Tin.

He took a final glance at Lady before stepping into the jungle to head for school. Y'Tin was always late. Always. The teacher, Monsieur Thorat, once paddled him on the legs for tardiness, but the paddle barely even stung. Monsieur was too nice to paddle anyone with force. And if he did give Y'Tin a hard paddling, Y'Tin knew his father would withdraw him from school. Sometimes Y'Tin wondered whether he should try to induce a hard paddling. Then he would get to stay home. On the other hand, it could be that his mother would just send him to a different school, one farther away and without such a patient teacher. And Monsieur Thorat actually knew an awful lot of useful and interesting information, but for some reason he hardly ever talked about it. For instance, Monsieur Thorat had told the class that in Thailand, American tourists paid elephant handlers for rides on their elephants. Y'Tin wondered how much an elephant ride cost. Monsieur Thorat had passed around a Thai magazine, and in it were pictures of painted elephants on parade. Y'Tin definitely would like to see that one day. And Thailand had not been dragged into the wars of Southeast Asia. That made Thailand even more interesting. Also, Monsieur Thorat had been to America. He said that Americans called a little rain a "storm" and called a storm a "torrent." He said Americans liked to visit other countries for "vacations." And he talked about "smog." He said most Americans worked inside buildings. Y'Tin wondered what that was like. He thought that it would kill him to work indoors every day. Anyway, as fascinating as Monsieur could be, he usually chose to be boring for reasons that would always be a mystery to Y'Tin.

Y'Tin tossed his book in the air and caught it as he walked. He had taken this path through the jungle countless times, but about halfway there he felt an odd fear, as if someone was watching him. He looked around but saw nothing unusual. This vague fear had been coming to him more and more often as North Vietnamese troops grew more aggressive about sending soldiers into South Vietnam. Supposedly, the Americans would take "severe retaliatory action" if the North Vietnamese broke what Monsieur Thorat called the 1973 Agreement on Ending the War and Restoring Peace in Vietnam, the treaty that ended American involvement in the war between North and South Vietnam. The meetings to discuss the agreement took place in Paris, and Ama always called them the Paris Peace Accords. All Y'Tin knew was that the North Vietnamese had broken the agreement and the Americans were nowhere to be seen. Y'Tin thought if they'd given the 1973 Agreement on Ending the War and Restoring Peace in Vietnam a shorter name— like the Paris Peace Treaty—the North Vietnamese would have followed it more. It was just a thought.

The school was a longhouse, which, unfortunately, had the only windows Y'Tin had ever seen. The reason this was unfortunate was that Y'Tin thought the view was more interesting than Monsieur Thorat, so it was hard to pay attention.

When he finally reached the school, he slipped into his chair and opened his book. Monsieur Thorat ignored him. Several boys were absent today. Y'Tin wanted to know why but sat attentively as Monsieur Thorat discussed nouns and verbs—now, *there* was something useful for an elephant keeper. A large part of class was conducted in French because the school had originally been set up when the French were here in the 1950s. But now the French were gone, and the only thing left of them was their language. There were English-speaking schools also, but Y'Tin didn't live near one and his mother did not want him living outside the village in order to go to school. Besides, she liked the French language. She even used a few French words like *bonjour*, *au revoir*, and *beaucoup*. *Beaucoup* was one of the favorite words of the Americans. They had used it all the time, because everything in this war was *beaucoup*: *beaucoup* soldiers, *beaucoup* weapons, and *beaucoup* deaths.

Monsieur Thorat turned to the class suddenly and said in Vietnamese, "I forgot to mention. I'm looking for an assistant in my house. My wife is pregnant and needs someone to help with our children."

"My sister will work for cows," Y'Tin offered.

"We have no cows."

35

"Chickens, then."

"We have no chickens."

Sometimes Y'Tin wondered how Monsieur Thorat survived. "Never mind then," Y'Tin said.

"Anyone who thinks they know someone interested, talk to me *after* class, please." The boys sat patiently while Monsieur Thorat wrote on the board. "Y'Tin!" he said crisply when he'd finished.

Y'Tin stood up. *"Bon matin,* Monsieur Thorat."

"Bon matin, Y'Tin. *Comment allez vous?"*

"Bien, Monsieur Thorat."

"Avez-vous fait vos devoirs?" Monsieur asked.

"Non. Je regrette, Monsieur Thorat."

Monsieur Thorat pursed his lips. Y'Tin had not even thought of his homework.

"Y'Juen, vos devoirs?"

"Non. Je regrette, Monsieur Thorat."

"Has *anybody* done their homework?" Monsieur Thorat cried out in Vietnamese.

Only Big Boy, from the Mnong tribe, raised a hand, causing Monsieur Thorat to purse his lips again. "Can anybody diagram this sentence?" he asked resignedly, as if he already knew the answer. Big Boy's hand raised again.

Gunfire sounded outside, and the entire class

fell to the ground. The classroom's only window shattered, shards of glass slicing through the air. Someone outside laughed.

Gunfire was nothing new. The war had been going on for as long as Y'Tin could remember. The French had fought in Vietnam before Y'Tin was born, and after that the Americans came, and left. And now the North and the South were fighting. The North was Communist, and the South was not, and that was supposedly the problem. Y'Tin didn't want the country to be Communist because then there would be too many rules. Life had enough rules as it was.

But his favorite auntie didn't like the Americans because several of the village men had been killed fighting with them. Auntie owned the longhouse and acted like the boss lady she was, but she had a deep belly laugh that always made Y'Tin laugh, even if he didn't know what he was laughing at. And since she owned all the family property, including Lady, Y'Tin respected her a lot. Still, he had liked the Americans. The Americans had been the only ones who'd treated the Dega as equals. His father said so over and over. And so, once again, it must be true.

Y'Tin waited for Monsieur to let the class know it was safe to rise. He idly jangled his brass bracelets. He saw that Y'Hon, who had no friends, was kneeling beneath his seat, reading. He was always reading, even when he walked. Y'Juen was watching a huge black spider crawl under his desk. Y'Juen was Y'Tin's best friend because they had been born on the same day, though in different years. They were in the same class because Y'Juen had started school one year after Y'Tin.

The boys stayed on the floor for several minutes before Monsieur Thorat stood up. "They're gone," he said.

"Who was it, Monsieur Thorat?" Y'Juen asked.

"I don't know," he replied, peering out the window.

Y'Tin stood up and peered out the window as well. Everything was peaceful outside. He guessed the temperature was about twenty-six degrees Celsius, the morning mist blown away and the sky as blue as he'd ever seen it. Y'Juen's family owned the only thermometer in the village. Now that there was a thermometer, everybody always wanted to know what the temperature was. Before, all you had to do was step outside to know if it was warm or cold. Now you needed a thermometer to tell you.

The wind drifted through the holes in the glass and brushed Y'Tin's face. It was actually a beautiful day.

Big Boy eagerly answered practically every question Monsieur Thorat asked the rest of the morning. He wasn't that smart, but he tried hardest. He was only second smartest, maybe third. Personally, Y'Tin felt he himself was second smartest. He just didn't get good grades. Why study? He was an elephant keeper!

Most of the afternoon was spent on math and language, and after school Y'Tin and a few of his friends walked home together. A strong wind had kicked up, rustling the towering trees. The canopy was so heavy and the trees were so tall that Y'Tin could not see the tops of many of them. Even an elephant looked small next to the trees. "I wonder what the shaman will say about the wind," Y'Tin remarked. The village shaman was an expert at studying the weather and what it meant.

"He's sick today," Y'Juen said. "His friends are going to sacrifice a pig to make him better."

"They should sacrifice the pig before he gets sick, not after."

"Now you think you're a shaman."

The boys laughed. Then Y'Juen grew serious.

"My father is talking about hiding in the jungle," he said. "He says the NVA is coming soon."

"My father said so too," Y'Tin said. He felt his stomach clench, the way it did sometimes when he thought about the war. His father had said that if the North Vietnamese Army took over South Vietnam by force, he would become a guerilla warrior based in the jungle. Monsieur Thorat had said that a guerilla was a soldier who was part of "an irregular armed force fighting a stronger force by sabotage and harassment." For instance, the Vietcong were the guerillas who fought on the same side as the North Vietnamese Army. Y'Tin had memorized the definition because it might be his own fate someday. Hopefully, that would never happen. The village was isolated in the jungle, and because of the heavy foliage, you could not even see the village from twenty steps away. It was possible the North Vietnamese might never even stumble across Y'Tin's home . . . or so he hoped.

Y'Tin continued, "Before they left, the Americans said they would help us."

"Help us what?" Y'Juen said.

Y'Tin thought that over. "Help us win the war. It's not too late." He knew that sounded ridiculous. They had not even won the war when the Americans *were* here.

"Why leave and come back when they were already here?"

All the boys stopped walking. Y'Tin looked at the others. He had known them since he was a baby. Why argue? And, more particularly, why argue when you knew you were wrong? So he suggested that they play soccer when they got home.

"Y'Tin, you can't even kick the ball straight," Y'Juen kidded him.

Y'Tin laughed. "Neither can you!"

By the time they reached the village, they were joking about who was the best soccer player. As usual, Lady was waiting for him. She liked to knock his head with her trunk when he returned home from school. That could actually be painful, but it made Y'Tin happy anyway. The other boys headed for the gate while Y'Tin unchained Lady. She looked up toward the sky as a helicopter roared above.

The helicopter passed exactly over where Y'Tin was standing, and he looked upward and waited for the noise to subside. When the Americans were here, helicopters passed overhead all the time. Y'Tin's mother had called it the War of the Helicopters. Y'Tin didn't recognize the make of the helicopter that flew overhead, but it might have been one that the Americans had left behind.

"Hey, Y'Tin," called out Tomas, sauntering up. "Did you learn anything in school today?"

"Nah. I already know everything." Tomas laughed, and they walked down to the river with Y'Siu and the elephants, as they did every day when Y'Tin got home. Y'Tin loved this part of the day. Next to his father, Tomas was the man Y'Tin most admired. Tomas knew elephants like nobody else, even Y'Tin.

"Someone shot up the window at school today," Y'Tin told them.

"Who was it?"

"I don't know. We heard them laugh."

"Maybe it was just a joke."

"Absolutely!" Y'Tin exclaimed.

Tomas put his hand on the top of his head and pulled it to the side, cracking his neck. He did that all the time. Y'Tin thought it was a strange habit, but what did he know?

Y'Tin watched the elephants walk silently

through the jungle. He felt sorry for all the animals, caught in the middle of a war. His father had told him that during one Special Forces mission they had come across several dead elephants where a bomb had dropped.

"If the North Vietnamese or Vietcong ever attack the village, we should escape with the elephants," Y'Tin said. His stomach hurt again.

"And if either you or Y'Siu gets hurt, I promise I'll bring your elephants into the jungle," Tomas replied.

"And if you get hurt, I'll take Geng with me when I escape with Lady, Y'Siu, and Dok. I swear it."

"I swear it too," Tomas said solemnly.

The jungle could soak up thousands of Dega villagers, "like a dry cloth soaking up water," according to Y'Tin's father. "We must use the jungle as a weapon," he liked to say. Every time he said that, he acted like it was the first time he'd said it, even though Y'Tin had heard him say the exact same thing at least ten times.

At the river, the elephants drank their fill and then loaded their trunks with water that they playfully sprayed into the air. Then they lumbered over to a bamboo grove and began pulling off leaves.

Y'Tin couldn't imagine eating nothing but leaves and grass and fruits—he would lose weight, absolutely. But the elephants grew huge from such a diet.

Y'Tin, Thomas, and Y'Siu squatted on the ground, Y'Tin trying to forget about the war. Right now is what he should be thinking of. The North Vietnamese might not even come to their village, he reminded himself again.

He turned his attention back to the elephants. They were ripping bark off a tree. The boys waited for the elephants to finish before taking them back.

When they returned to the pen, Tomas cleaned it up while Y'Siu stroked and talked to and chanted to Dok. He did that a lot. Sometimes Y'Siu had whole conversations with his elephant. Y'Tin headed for the gate. The women had left the fields to make the evening meal, and he could smell meat cooking. Outside the fence, Y'Tin's friends were still kicking around a soccer ball. Y'Tin broke into a run and gave the ball the hardest kick he could. For once the ball flew through the air and landed ten meters away.

"Y'Tin hit the ball straight!" shouted Y'Juen. "It's a miracle!"

"You're just jealous!" Y'Tin shouted back.

Some of the older boys walked through their game. "Nobody's jealous of you!" one of them shouted out. Y'Tin watched Y'Juen chase after the boys. Y'Juen was always worried about what the older boys thought. He was insecure that way. On the other hand, he was physically brave. He once jumped from a tall waterfall into the river below. Y'Tin wouldn't make the jump—he was too scared. But Y'Tin didn't care what the older boys thought. Let them think what they wanted. That had nothing to do with him.

They played until the men came in from the fields. As Y'Tin headed for his longhouse, Y'Pioc, one of the older boys, ran up to him. "Y'Tin! Wait up."

Y'Tin waited. Y'Pioc said, "Say, did you hear? My family and yours have decided I'm going to marry your sister in three years." Y'Pioc was fifteen years old, as was Y'Tin's sister H'Juaih. His sister was a catch because Y'Tin's family owned a beautiful gong, an elephant, twenty buffalo, countless chickens, and numerous jars of fermenting rice wine buried in the ground. And his family's farmlands were more extensive than any other family's in the village. Anyway, Y'Pioc was quiet, but Y'Tin liked him.

Y'Tin could tell that all three of his spirits were content and that he would make H'Juaih happy. It was a good marriage for both sides. H'Juaih wasn't as pretty as some girls, but everybody agreed she was one of the smartest. And there was something about her, a kind of grace, that also made her a good catch. When the time came, Y'Pioc would move in with Y'Tin's family, and not long after that Y'Tin would move in with whomever he married. Y'Tin would miss his family, but that was the way it was.

Y'Tin's parents had been talking about H'Juaih for several months. As usual, it took Ama a long time to make a decision. Since boys always became a part of the wife's family, Ama had been concerned that Y'Pioc wouldn't fit in with the family, but last night after some begging from H'Juaih, Ama had finally decided that it was a good match.

"Congratulations," Y'Tin said.

"When we're brothers, can you teach me how to take care of elephants?"

People said that Y'Tin liked elephants more than he liked people, which was true. And Y'Tin knew that some people thought he could talk with the elephants. Y'Tin often laid his forehead against Lady's hide, and he felt he did sort of talk with her. That was the truth. Still, he was no match for Y'Siu. During Y'Siu's long conversations with Dok, he would occasionally pause, as if listening to his elephant.

Y'Tin laughed. "You might start to like elephants more than my sister. She'll have to compete for attention."

They both laughed. "But seriously, you'll teach me?"

"Whenever you want. You're my family now. That's the truth."

"Do you need me to help you today?"

"No," Y'Tin said. "But you can come with me to wash her one morning before school if you want."

He saw his sister walking with some friends past the small longhouse of the Knul clan. Y'Pioc ran after them, trailing the girls without speaking. Y'Tin watched until they walked out of sight. Y'Tin was happy for his sister. She and Y'Pioc could both be a little prim, but maybe marriage would loosen them up.

When he reached his house, Y'Tin climbed up the ladder. An elephant was carved at the top. Everywhere Y'Tin looked, he saw elephants. That was his fate.

Chapter Four

H is mother was boiling rice and jungle potatoes in the kitchen outside their bedroom.
Chickens, buffalo, and pigs were mostly
used for sacrifices rather than for daily meals. Meat
to consume for dinner came from hunting and the
various fish and small-animal traps Y'Tin and his
father set in the jungle. All down the long hallway,
Y'Tin saw women cooking at their kitchens. All
ten women cooked with great solemnity, as if they
were involved in a very serious matter. His auntie
who owned the longhouse was no doubt cooking
chicken. Y'Tin's family could have eaten chicken
too, but Y'Tin's mother didn't believe in eating meat
every night because despite the family's wealth,

she was very frugal. Y'Tin remembered that the Americans were so rich, they ate meat every day.

"How was school?" his mother asked. Her hair was tied back the way it always was when she was cooking. She was taller than his father, and her face was smooth and round. She wiped her hands on her sarong and looked at him.

"Ah, school. It was—honestly, Ami, it was the same as always. One day is like the next."

"Go study until we eat," she scolded him. She turned back to her cooking.

"Ami, you're . . . you're the best mother in the village, no joke," Y'Tin said. He took a step closer to her to get her attention.

"Did you go to school?" she asked without looking up.

"Yes, of course."

"If I find out you're lying to me, I'll beat you with a stick."

Y'Tin laughed. "You never beat me with a stick before. Anyway, like I was saying, you're the best mother in any village anywhere."

"What do you want, Y'Tin?" His mother sighed. She looked at him again. "You're up to something." But she said it affectionately.

"Ami, like I said, you're the best mother in history. I appreciate that. But, see, there's . . . I can study books while I sit with the elephants, but I can't take care of the elephants while I'm at school. So, because, ah, well, because I can learn while I stay at home but I can't take care of the elephants while I'm at school, ah, there's no reason for me to go to school!" he finished emphatically. She didn't reply, just returned to her cooking. He shrugged and went to his family's room to throw down his schoolbook. He could just be losing his mind, but he really thought he was making progress with his mother.

Once in a great while, when Y'Tin went hunting with his father, he was allowed to stay home from school. Otherwise, his mother was firm in her refusal to let him quit. He had ditched school three times, but each time she found out because H'Juaih had told on him. All three times Ami had looked like she wanted to cry, which was punishment enough to make him go to school as often as he could stand it.

Y'Tin wandered out to the front porch to see if anything interesting was going on outside. One of the chickens was on the porch. He hadn't even noticed when he'd climbed up. "There's a chicken out here!" he called to his mother.

"It's sick," she called back. "Leave it alone."

He climbed down the notches of the ladder and clucked for the chickens. They came running, and he opened up their coop so they could go inside.

Later, at dinner, Y'Tin closed his eyes and thanked the spirits for the food and also asked for safety for his family and his tribe's elephants.

His family sat on mats on the floor. For reasons no one had ever explained to Y'Tin, men ate with chopsticks and women ate with their hands. Y'Tin bopped his younger sister on the head with a chopstick as his mother watched, half amused and half annoyed. "Stop that, Y'Tin," she said mildly. His little sister's name was H'Lir, but they all called her Jujubee for the jujube candy that Shepard's wife used to send him from home. H'Lir had loved the candy so much that she once ate two whole boxes in one sitting.

She opened her eyes wide at Y'Tin, then crossed them. "Ami, Jujubee is crossing her eyes again," Y'Tin said.

"Stop that," his mother told her. "You'll have crossed eyes when you're old if you don't stop it. Don't tempt the spirits."

"The spirits won't punish *me*. I'm only . . . I'm . . ."

"Five," Y'Tin said. "You know that."

"I forgot."

Y'Tin hit her on the head again. "That'll clear your brain up."

His mother handed Ama a bowl of food, then told the others to serve themselves. Y'Tin spooned rice and potatoes into his bowl.

His father nodded gravely at nothing in particular as he picked at his rice. "Maybe they'll get us extra guns somehow," he murmured, his mind elsewhere. When Y'Tin's father said "they," he always meant the Americans. Y'Tin knew that the Special Forces had left them weapons, many of which the tribe had buried in the jungle.

Y'Tin was about to ask his father about that when he suddenly realized that he could smell elephant meat cooking. Ordinarily, he did not have a particularly good sense of smell, but something about cooking elephant meat made him retch. "Did somebody catch an elephant?" he asked his mother. He sniffed at the air. It didn't smell much different from any other meat, but for Y'Tin there was something sickly about it.

"Yes, the Nie clan killed a small wild elephant and is having a feast with some friends. We weren't invited, of course." People who owned elephants never ate them. Once last year when one of the clans feasted on an elephant, Y'Tin threw a silent curse on them. Several weeks later four of the kids got sick with malaria. Y'Tin felt so guilty, he resolved never to throw a curse again.

After dinner he went moodily to his family's room and sulked with his back against a wall. Why kill an elephant when the jungle was full of deer and the rivers were full of fish? The rest of his family had moved to the front porch, so he was alone in the room. He leaned back, trying to get the smell out of his nostrils.

Suddenly, Jujubee came flying into the room, knocking his head against the wall. Jujubee always did things with twice the energy that was needed. She laughed energetically, she cried energetically, she pouted energetically, and she worked energetically.

"Watch it!" he cried out. He felt the back of his head. "I think my head is broken!"

Jujubee began to cry. "You don't love me!" That's what she said almost every time anyone scolded her.

"I love you, but my head is broken."

She ran out of the room. "You don't love me!"

He could hear the sound of raised voices. He got up to see what was going on. On the porch his parents were having an argument. "I'm not leaving the village," his mother was saying. "They can kill me if they want, but I'm not leaving. This is my home."

"You'll feel differently if they come here," his father insisted. "Don't assume the spirits will smile on you just because you've never crossed them."

"Why would anyone kill me? I didn't work for the Americans."

"But I did!" his father cried, raising his voice to a shout.

That argument again. They'd had it several times. Y'Tin said, "Later, gator!" and climbed down the ladder. He loved the way the Americans talked, he really did.

At the pen the elephants were nibbling on a mound of grass Tomas had cut for them. Y'Tin unchained Lady and led her to the edge of the jungle so she could eat more. She chewed on fresh grass and then suddenly reached out and pulled down a tree with her trunk. Y'Tin scrambled out of the way as the tree crashed down. Her trunk could pick up a pebble as easily as it could pull down a tree. He always thought of the trunk as being at the center of an elephant, just as the heart was the center of a human. Sometimes, when Lady was especially happy to see him, she wrapped her trunk around him and squeezed, knocking the air out of him. He should probably scold her for that, but he didn't want her to think he didn't love her. Tomas thought that was ridiculous reasoning, but Y'Tin didn't care.

Y'Tin heard his name being called and turned around. H'Juaih was running through the sugarcane field with her arms flapping through the air. He ran toward her.

"What is it?" he said, taking hold of her arm.

"Ama wants you." She held on to a lock of her long hair, the way she always did when she was worried or thinking.

"What does he want?"

"I don't know. He said it was important and for me to hurry. He said, 'Why does that boy always rush off to his elephant when there are important matters to discuss?'"

"They were arguing," he defended himself. "Tomas! Can you keep an eye on Lady?"

Tomas raised a few fingers in reply.

Y'Tin and H'Juaih trotted together around the family's field. The green shoots were tiny and vulnerable. Sometimes his parents slept outside with the crops, to catch vermin that might eat them.

Now the crescent moon hung over the village in the still-blue sky. One of Y'Tin's uncles believed that a daytime moon was luckier than a nighttime moon. Y'Tin had no opinion about that; he would have to study it further one day.

H'Juaih and Y'Tin slipped through the village gate. At the closest longhouse he saw one of the families holding a small ritual, just a chicken and one jar of rice wine. Probably someone was a little sick, so they were sacrificing a chicken. Several men were sipping from the jar with long straws. One of them stopped to say loudly, "I'll fight the Vietcong with my bare hands if I have to." He slurred his words, and Y'Tin knew he'd been drinking quite a bit.

Y'Tin's father was waiting outside their longhouse. The stilts at the front entrance were slanting, making the inside of the house slant as well. That was because his addled uncle (who had come from the Knul clan) helped construct that part of the house.

He'd insisted on being in charge of building. He and Y'Tin's youngest aunt had divorced a couple of years ago, and he had gone back to live with the Knuls. The Knuls had a reputation for being oddballs. Y'Tin had no idea why his family had allowed his auntie to marry a Knul. Anyway, the house still slanted. That was the story Ami had told him about why the house was that way. She had been lecturing him on how he was supposed to behave someday when he went to live in his wife's house. Uncle, she'd told Y'Tin, was an example of everything Y'Tin should not be.

There was nowhere private inside, so Ama gestured Y'Tin to follow him. They usually talked in private out by the tobacco fields or, when Ama was in a hurry, at the fence on the far south side of the village. Tonight Y'Tin followed his father to the fence. He knew his father had been thinking. Whenever he'd been thinking, it often seemed to involve Y'Tin. That's because H'Juaih was perfect and Jujubee was still young.

Y'Tin peeked through an opening in the fence and could see the elephants beyond the fields. Lady was dragging the tree that she'd knocked down. She always liked to play with her food. "Forget the elephants for a moment," Ama said shortly.

Y'Tin looked at his father with surprise. He knew his father took great pride in Y'Tin's expertise about elephants.

"Y'Tin, some of the men have been talking about moving into the jungle and setting up a guerilla encampment."

"But you've been talking about it since the Americans left."

"We used to speak of it casually, but now we speak of it seriously."

So many Dega tribesmen had worked closely with the American Special Forces that all might be considered guilty if caught by either the North Vietnamese or the Vietcong. Their lives were all at risk if and when the village was overrun by the enemy. Y'Tin was going to reason this out the way his father would. Some people felt that the women would be safer if the men left the villages. In fact, Y'Tin had heard that to the east, men had abandoned several villages for life in the jungle.

Y'Tin's father prodded him. "Do you understand what I'm saying?"

"You might be moving away?"

"We *will* be moving away."

And even though Y'Tin had heard this before,

his father's tone was so ominous that Y'Tin felt a jolt of fear run down his spine. If his father said it, it was of course true. Y'Tin frowned and looked down, and at that exact moment an enormous cockroach scurried between him and his father. Maybe that was a good sign, but maybe not—he and his father were being split in two by the path of the bug.

Y'Tin knew that in a fight between North and South, the North would win. That was the only certainty. Without the Americans, the South Vietnamese had a weaker army than the North did. Some South Vietnamese soldiers were already surrendering, but the Dega tribes would continue the war regardless of what the South Vietnamese Army did.

In addition to collaborating with the Special Forces, many Dega had joined the South Vietnam Rangers after the U.S. withdrawal. His father had worked for three years with the Americans. But when the Americans left, he had returned to farming and hunting.

"Is South Vietnam going to surrender soon?" Y'Tin asked.

"Whether they'll surrender or whether they'll simply be overrun, I don't know the answer to that. But whatever happens will happen soon."

His father was just thirty-three, but his face was crisscrossed with lines. Despite the approaching dusk, his lines looked even more severe than usual. For some reason Y'Tin looked at his father's hands. The veins ran like welts up his hands and wrists and then up his arms.

"How soon, Ama?" asked Y'Tin.

"Any day. Maybe next year. Maybe tomorrow. And anytime in between."

"But, Ama . . ." To Y'Tin's own ears, his voice came out like a whine. He tried to formulate what he wanted to say. "But, Ama, everybody has said 'any day' since the Special Forces left."

His father took Y'Tin's shoulders in his hands. "Y'Tin, you have to face what's happening. You're almost a man. The North Vietnamese might put you in a reeducation camp."

Y'Tin's stomach hurt. A reeducation camp was where the North Vietnamese put you to strip your identity and to teach you to be a good Communist. Y'Tin did not want to be reeducated. He already knew everything he needed to know. He turned to peek at the elephants again. Lady was looking toward the fence, as though she knew exactly where he was. He turned back to his father, who was gazing sternly at him.

"I'm not scared."

"Then you're not thinking straight," his father snapped. "I wanted to tell you that at some point you and your friends will need to take the elephants into the jungle. Stay there."

"How long should I stay there?"

"Until I get word to you."

"But how will you find me?"

Y'Tin's father did not take his eyes off of him. "I don't know yet. I've never been in this situation before."

"But . . ." If Ama didn't know, then there was nobody left to ask. "What do you mean? Do you mean . . . you don't know?" Y'Tin waited for more, but Ama had stopped to think. He liked to think so much that he'd taught himself how to read just so he could learn new ideas. Y'Tin waited a moment for his father to speak again. When Ama didn't speak, Y'Tin asked, "What about Ami? What about H'Juaih and Jujubee?"

"Your mother must leave, and even if she does not, I have to. It's our only chance."

"But she'll need you to protect her."

"With a crossbow?"

"But, Ama, the Americans said they would help us. Shepard promised. It must be that they don't know what's going on." Y'Tin paused, then said excitedly, "We need to get a message to them." His father sometimes spoke of the Americans coming back, but he hadn't spoken of it lately.

"Y'Tin, they said they would help us two years ago. And what have they done? The Americans aren't coming back, and I say that with certainty."

Y'Tin stared into his father's eyes. His gaze was steely. Y'Tin looked away first. Now he knew for sure: The Americans weren't coming back. "When will you leave, Ama?"

"We're having a meeting about it tomorrow."

"Can I come?"

"Of course."

"I'm not going back to school anymore."

"Your mother doesn't expect you to. I just spoke with her. Now go on to your elephant."

Y'Tin turned to leave, but his father put his hand on Y'Tin's shoulder again. "I would die for your mother. But the reality is that dying would not help her."

"You can kill a man with a crossbow."

"Killing one man means nothing when there are a hundred men. Now go on." His eyes softened and he tousled Y'Tin's hair. Then he strode toward the longhouse.

Y'Tin paused at the gate and gazed at the village. It seemed so utterly peaceful. Y'Thon Nie, who was in his older sister's class, was clucking to his family's chickens. The sun was setting on the west side of the fence. Tomas's mother was tending her special eggplants in their garden. Nobody knew how her eggplants grew so delicious. She wouldn't tell anyone her secret. Y'Tin had no secrets at all, but his mother had many. For instance, she wouldn't tell anyone if she'd loved anyone before she married Ama. And she wouldn't tell anyone how she cooked her special buffalo stew.

Anyway, Y'Tin could still smell elephant meat. That seemed like a bad omen. As he crossed through the fields, he saw Lady grow fidgety as she spotted him. She walked toward him but stopped, exactly at the point where she would have had to stop had she been chained. He hoped she didn't try to cross the field. His parents would scold him for not chaining her . . . or maybe they wouldn't. They had more important things to worry about now.

On the way to the elephant pen Y'Tin again had the sensation that someone was watching him. He looked around and saw nothing. Then he looked anxiously at the jungle. The sensation was so strong that he paused. Still nothing. He continued to the pen. He snapped off a piece of bamboo for Lady, but she wasn't interested. With her amazing sense of smell, she probably knew the Nies were eating elephant meat.

He lay on his back as the first *mtu* appeared in the sky, sparkling shyly. The war was coming just like the *mtu* came, barely sparkling at first and then glowing stronger and stronger. And then as darkness came, all you could see were the *mtu*. He listened to the leaves in the jungle rustling with the wind. He loved the sound suddenly. He loved the wind on his face. He loved lying on the ground quietly. Tomas, Y'Siu, and Y'Tin liked to lie on the ground near the elephants because it felt risky but also comforting. The elephants could step on them—but they wouldn't. That was elephants for you.

The next morning Y'Tin awoke to the rising sun, and his first thought was that he hadn't done his homework again and, as a matter of fact, couldn't quite remember what his homework was.

Then he remembered that he didn't have to go to school today and might never have to go to school again. And all of a sudden, he actually *wanted* to go to school. School had been predictable, but now he *wanted* a predictable life.

"Did you hear the gunfire last night?" Tomas asked. Tomas spent about half his nights sleeping near the elephants and the other half in his long-house with his family. Y'Siu approached and sat down without even a greeting. That was his way.

Y'Tin shook his head. Y'Tin hadn't heard anything. The first time he had heard gunfire in the distance, he was surprised how harmless it sounded.

"My father says there's a meeting of the whole village today," Tomas said.

"Yes, I've heard. Are you scared?" Y'Tin asked.

"No . . . yes. Yes, I am. What about you?"

"Yes. I just want the war to be over. Then we can go back to our regular lives." Yet even as Y'Tin spoke, he knew he was wrong. They would never go back to their regular lives.

Y'Siu climbed to the top of Y'Tin's hutch and slid across Dok's back. Then the three of them took the elephants down the wide path to the river. At the river the elephants drank and drank the way they did every morning. Elephants could drink two hundred liters a day. That took a while.

"I'm not leaving without the elephants," Y'Siu announced.

No one replied. Of course Y'Tin wouldn't leave without the elephants either. But where would they go? After drinking their fill, the elephants wandered over to a bamboo grove, where Lady picked young shoots and then pushed them around on the ground for a few minutes before eating them. Usually, Y'Tin was the last to leave the river, but this time the others lingered as well. Y'Siu lay atop Dok. Suddenly, tears were falling down his face. Though Y'Siu was fifteen, Y'Tin always thought of him as the youngest. His voice hadn't changed yet, and you always had to be careful what you said to him because you might hurt his feelings.

Y'Tin and Tomas glanced at each other, then Y'Tin said, "It's okay, Y'Siu."

"I'm scared." He was sobbing now.

"We're all scared," Tomas said. "Everyone is scared. Our fathers are scared. Our grandfathers are scared. The chief is scared."

"Y'Siu, we'll live in the jungle. We know how to

hunt. We'll be safe," Y'Tin said, trying to comfort Y'Siu. Anyway, it was possible that they would be safe.

"I don't want to live in the jungle. I want to stay here with Dok."

The elephants finished eating before Y'Siu finished crying.

Back at the pen Tomas said, "Don't chain your elephants. If the enemy comes, the elephants may need to flee into the jungle."

"Go ahead and wander, Lady," said Y'Tin. He patted her pregnant belly. "I'll be right back." But he knew she wouldn't wander. She would walk only as far as her chain would have let her. She was so domesticated, he worried that she might not be able to survive in the jungle if something happened to him. For the first time in his life, he regretted that Lady had ever been captured.

Y'Tin, Tomas, and Y'Siu walked across the empty fields. Y'Tin had never seen the fields like that in the morning. Everybody always started working before Y'Tin headed for school. The Rhade prided themselves on how hard they worked. Their whole lives revolved around working. But that didn't matter now.

Chapter Five

Y'Tin had expected to find all the villagers talking animatedly about the big meeting. Instead, an eerie silence had fallen like ashes from the sky. The yellow, grass roofs of the houses shivered in the wind. The private gardens and rice paddies were unattended, and nobody seemed to have remembered to let their chickens out. Usually at this time of morning, chickens were clucking everywhere.

At his own house Y'Tin found everyone gathered on the floor of the large room at the entrance. All his relatives had closed their eyes and were holding hands. He had never seen this before, so he did not think it was a ritual. It was more like they could not stand to face the world at this moment.

He sat down. Jujubee immediately came over and leaned against him. Apparently, she'd gotten a nosebleed, for a small piece of cloth was sticking out of her right nostril. She was usually full of energy, but when she got nosebleeds, she suddenly grew docile and wanted to lie on Y'Tin. Ami kept a supply of small pieces of cloth handy for when Jujubee got one of her frequent nosebleeds.

"Is it a bad one?" Y'Tin asked Jujubee.

"Yes, we've had to change the cloth four times."

He put his arms around her and pulled her in close.

A gong sounded, but at first nobody moved. It was as if no gong had rung at all. His mother did not even open her eyes. Then Y'Tin's father stood up, and everyone except his mother followed. As the others headed down the ladder, Y'Tin stood uncertainly. "Ami?" he said. "We're going."

Finally, she opened her eyes. She pushed herself up slowly, as if she were an old woman. Y'Tin waited until Jujubee and Ami had climbed down the ladder. He gazed around the room.

He needed to soak in the moment, to remember his house. Then he headed to the meeting by himself.

Y'Tin watched the men pour out of the bachelor longhouse. Some of them were old, in their late thirties. He wondered whether it might be better in times of war to have no family to worry about. But he couldn't imagine having no family.

The meeting was being held outside because the entire village of five hundred would not fit into the meeting hall. Y'Tin sat in the front because he wanted to see the proceedings up close. The shaman sat near him with his stick. It looked just like a plain stick such as you might find lying on the ground in the jungle. But that was only a disguise. The shaman used this amazing stick to communicate with the spirits. No doubt it would be the stick that would tell them what kind of sacrifices they would need to make today.

The shaman was tall for a Rhade. He was almost as tall as the Americans had been. He was lean except for his stomach, which formed a small mound, like when Y'Tin's mother was first pregnant with Jujubee. But his face was what Y'Tin studied now. One eye was bigger than the other, and his mouth curled up more on one side than the other. The result was otherworldly.

Some of the men somberly smoked pipes. Y'Tin overheard two old women talking of making a sacrifice to Yang Lie, the great evil spirit. Once, last year, Yang Lie had chased Y'Tin down—Y'Tin had sprained an ankle tripping over a rock one week, and the next week he'd sprained a wrist tripping over another rock. His parents had sacrificed a couple of chickens to Yang Lie, and then Y'Tin didn't get hurt again. So he knew that Yang Lie was susceptible to sacrifices.

The Rhade spent much of their time thinking about the spirits. Every living and nonliving thing was inhabited by at least one spirit, so you had to watch your step all the time. Sometimes his mother worried so much about the spirits that she couldn't sleep at night. Every so often Y'Tin liked to boil an egg and give it as a private sacrifice for his family. So far it seemed to be working, since his family had been prospering for several years. His family was very lucky indeed.

The village chief, dressed head to toe in khaki army clothes, arrived and scowled at the crowd. Everyone fell silent. The chief was very dramatic, and his face was rarely at rest. He gestured a lot when he talked. It was just his way. He could be talking about, say, whether to eat eggplant or corn at dinner, and he would gesture dramatically and talk very loudly. In fact, his nickname among the boys was Monsieur Loud. Now he cleared his throat and shouted out, "Many of us have been talking informally about what our next move should be. According to our own spies, the North Vietnamese are nearing our village. Every day they are in violation of the Paris Peace Accords, and yet the Americans still don't come to offer us aid." He leaned forward and paused dramatically. Y'Tin found himself leaning forward too. "We will now ask the shaman for advice about where to go, how much to take, and when to go."

Y'Tin waited for the shaman to ask the stick. "Asking the stick" meant that the shaman would ask his stick for advice. It was a special stick, and the spirits would speak to him through its movement. He would hold out the stick in front of him, and he would concentrate as the stick shook. Once, one of the Americans drank a lot of rice wine and tried to explain why asking the stick didn't make sense. But it made perfect sense to Y'Tin. How was it different from what the Americans said about electricity? The power in electricity went through a wire. In the same way, the power of the spirits went through the stick. Simple.

And the village boasted one of the most talented shamans around. Sometimes visitors from other villages made the long trek here to ask the shaman for advice. Y'Tin was pretty proud to live in the same village with such a talented shaman. Now the shaman raised his stick as if his arms were magically floating up, and for all Y'Tin knew, they really *were* magically floating up. The dark part of his eyes disappeared, leaving only white balls for eyes. Y'Tin sat very still, staring at those eyeballs. The chief asked loudly, "What should we sacrifice to appease the spirits?"

The shaman's tongue stretched out of his mouth and wriggled. Once, the shaman's tongue had grown so long, it reached the ground. Y'Tin had not seen it, but he knew several people who had. The shaman brought in his tongue, and his eyes normalized. His hands, which held the stick, began to shake. This went on for quite a while. And then it went on for quite a while longer. Y'Tin had never seen it go on so long. Finally, the stick stopped shaking. Y'Tin could not hear a single noise from any of the five hundred people present.

"You should leave the village within two days," the shaman finally said. "Women, children, and the elderly should leave as well. That is the message of Ai Die, great spirit of the sky, most powerful of the spirits, ruler of our world. Each family should sacrifice a buffalo if they have one, a pig if they don't have a buffalo, and a chicken if they don't have a pig." Then it was as if the shaman turned back into a normal man again.

When he turned normal, everyone jumped up at once, all running madly here and there. Y'Tin sought out his father and asked him urgently, "What should I do?"

"Dig up the rice wine," Ama said, then turned his attention to the other men in the family.

Y'Tin ran toward his house.

The clan's many big jars of rice wine were fermenting beneath the ground under and around the house. That was the way to let the wine ferment perfectly, or so Y'Tin had been told. Y'Tin used his hands to dig the jars out of the ground. He dug like a dog, kneeling on his knees and digging one hand quickly after the other, dirt flying

74

everywhere. He didn't know how many jars his father wanted, but he decided to dig up all twenty of the jars. If they were leaving in two days, they might as well drink what they could before they had to leave it all behind. Y'Tin concentrated on his task, as if his family's life depended on how quickly he could dig out the jars. While his body was busy digging, his mind was busy thinking. Where would they all go? Would they ever return to their village? How long would they need to hide in the jungle? Would he be able to take good care of the elephants? Would they all stick together, or would they all spread out?

When he saw the men in his clan carrying a dead buffalo to the longhouse, Y'Tin paused. Blood poured out of the animal's lungs. Y'Tin watched as his father started a fire with one of the lighters he had bought during his last trip to the biggest Rhade city of Ban Me Thuot. One of his uncles began slicing the buffalo into sections.

As Y'Tin was finishing the digging, the scent of roasting buffalo filled the air. Y'Tin did not feel even slightly hungry. He told his father he was going to the elephant pen. As if they had all read one another's minds, Y'Tin, Tomas, and Y'Siu were walking through the gate at nearly the same time. Y'Tin called out, "Tomas!"

Tomas waited for him impatiently. "Hurry!" Tomas yelled, and then he suddenly turned around and began running toward the elephants, leaving Y'Tin behind. Y'Tin ran as well, and Y'Siu followed. It was a good time to take the elephants for another drink at the river. Y'Tin saw that the elephants had not strayed from their pen.

It would feel good to walk to the river. Normal. Y'Tin found he loved the thought of doing something normal.

"What do you think would happen if we all stayed in the village?" asked Y'Tin. "*I* never worked for the Americans."

"But your father did," Tomas said neutrally. "And Y'Siu's father did. Anyway, how would the enemy know who worked for the Special Forces or not? They might suspect all of us because of a few—" He stopped, and Y'Tin wondered what he had planned on saying. To Geng, Tomas said, "*Nao!*" Geng immediately began the trek to the river. Geng was very obedient, but she listened only to Tomas.

Suddenly, they heard shouting. Y'Tin's sister

and Tomas's mother were racing across the field crying out, "Hurry! The North Vietnamese have been spotted nearby. The chief says everyone must leave immediately."

Y'Tin sprinted toward them. "What? What, *now*?" he asked.

"Ama said we need to leave now!" H'Juaih burst into tears.

Y'Tin grabbed her hand, and they ran back to their longhouse. Their father was stuffing canteens into a bag. He turned to Y'Tin and said angrily, "Go take care of your elephant. Go now."

H'Juaih screeched at him, "He said to go! Ama said to go *now*!"

For a moment Y'Tin couldn't move. "But what about Ami and Jujubee?"

"I've taken care of them," Ama said, slowly this time, as if Y'Tin had a learning impairment. "You need to go now."

So Y'Tin grabbed his crossbow, all seven arrows he owned, and a beautiful woven bag that his mother had made for him. *"Now!"* H'Juaih cried. She grabbed an empty bag and spun around as if she didn't have the slightest idea what to put in the bag. She tried to run down the steps, falling down the last two. The pathways were strangely empty, but Y'Tin could hear shouting inside the longhouses. He rushed behind his sister, but at the gate they both paused. "Travel safely," she said.

"Travel safely," he said.

He ran toward the elephant pen and she toward the jungle.

He was the first one back to the pen, but he did not wait for Y'Siu or Tomas. His father had said to leave *now*. If his father said it, then it must be done. He grabbed everything he kept in the hutch: the special brush for washing Lady, a pipe his grandfather had given him, rope, and his hook. He rammed the hook into Geng's leg. *"Nao!"* Next he jabbed Dok. *"Nao!"* he cried. *"Nao!"* Dok hurried off, but Geng did not. Y'Tin rammed Geng's leg one more time. He threw the rope around Lady's neck, tied the bag to her, then scrambled to the roof of his hutch and slid across to Lady's back. *"Nao,"* he said. He poked her with the hook, but she hesitated, no doubt surprised at the poke. *"Nao!"* She broke into a trot toward the jungle. He looked back at Geng, still waiting for Tomas.

Y'Tin heard murmuring, then realized it was himself, murmuring in English, "I'm okay. I'm okay." He looked back toward the gate and saw people pouring out of the gateway, as if they had all finished shouting in their houses at the same time and now were all rushing toward the jungle at the same time. He thought he spotted his favorite auntie, but it was hard to tell in the rush of people. His heart started to pound. He wondered whether his father's heart was pounding as well. Maybe Ama was so brave that his heart never pounded at all.

Y'Tin's heart went directly from pounding to stopping, for Jujubee was crying all alone by the fence. He slipped off Lady and jabbed her with the hook. "*Nao*, Lady! *Nao!*" he cried out. She hurried away. He had to check to make sure Jujubee was taken care of. He just had to.

He ran toward the fence, tripping twice. He was running as fast as he could, but it seemed to take forever to span the distance to his little sister. As soon as he made the turn for the gate, he dropped to the ground in fear. North Vietnamese soldiers swarmed all over the gate like ants. Y'Tin got up again and started to run, but a soldier shouted, "Stop! Stop! Lie down!" Y'Tin fell to the ground and braced himself as he saw a foot lowering.

Pow—it smashed against his nose. Ah, the pain in his face was excruciating. "Don't move!" said a voice that sounded almost like a girl's. Y'Tin froze; he felt desperate to stay alive. Surely this soldier must have more important things to attend to, but he was focusing on Y'Tin for some reason. Y'Tin peeked up and saw that the soldier seemed even younger than him. Maybe he didn't know what else to do other than harass another kid.

Then he became aware that the whole village was erupting. Guns were firing and people were running into the jungle and so many people were shouting that Y'Tin couldn't quite figure out what was going on. When he tried to turn his head to look, the boy soldier's foot crashed against his face again, making a strange cracking sound. Y'Tin wondered dazedly whether his nose or cheekbone was broken. His whole face hurt. He lay there, not moving, not knowing what was going on.

Finally the village grew quieter, and all the shouting was now coming from only the North Vietnamese—Y'Tin could tell by the accents. What did that mean? Did that mean the North Vietnamese had taken over the village? He felt dizzy and needed to close his eyes. He murmured as before, "I'm okay.

I'm okay." Then he braced himself again, turned his head, and opened his eyes . . . and saw the butt of a rifle smash down repeatedly on the head of one of the village bachelors. Blood and brains spurted out of his skull. "Ah," Y'Tin grunted. He retched and needed to close his eyes.

"Boys and men over here!" shouted a soldier from inside the fence. "Now!"

The boy soldier kicked Y'Tin more softly this time. "Go on. Get up," he said. When Y'Tin got up, the boy was suddenly angry. "Go on!" he cried out. "Get inside the gate!"

Y'Tin hurried through the gate, the boy pushing the rifle into his back the whole time. He saw some of the Ayŭns and the Buonyas and the Krongs, but he did not see any of his family. He thought that was a good sign . . . wasn't it? It meant his family had escaped . . . didn't it? A rifle jabbed his stomach. "Pay attention!" someone told him. The boy soldier had disappeared.

Y'Tin tried to strike a subservient pose. He knew that all he had to do was wear the wrong expression and he could be shot.

Another soldier—there were so many of them!—ran over to the one who appeared to be in charge. "That house is big enough," he said, pointing to the Buonya longhouse.

"All right, put them all in there," said the man in charge. "Check it for weapons and food first."

A couple of soldiers cleared the Buonya longhouse of guns, ammunition, and food. Y'Tin was shocked at how many guns they'd owned—maybe ten or twelve.

Y'Tin looked around wildly for his family or any of his friends. But he was all alone. A pretty girl smiled at one of the soldiers, who smiled back. Y'Tin stared in surprise at the girl. She was one of the shyest girls in the village, but you would never guess it at that moment. Y'Tin could see that beneath her smile was terror, and a will to live no matter what it took, no matter if it took smiling at the soldiers, or more.

Meanwhile, a boy named Y'Elur eagerly told the soldiers, "What do you need? I'll help you." Scared as Y'Tin was of what would happen next, he could not bring himself to be like Y'Elur. Still, he looked for an opportunity to endear himself to the soldiers. For some reason he seemed to have started out on the wrong foot, especially with the boy soldier. He spotted Y'Juen suddenly, as if he had appeared out of nowhere. His heart speeded up. They locked eyes for a moment. Y'Tin felt a huge relief to see someone he was close to, but then he felt guilty that he had felt glad to see him. He ought to have felt more glad *not* to see him, *not* to see anyone he was close to.

The Buonya longhouse became a jail as the soldiers herded the villagers inside. Before Y'Tin went inside, he stole a glance at some of the soldiers. They were very thin and very young. There may have been one hundred of them, which equaled one hundred guns. The oldest one looked like he was about nineteen or twenty. Y'Tin climbed up the Buonya ladder. Everyone was pushing their way toward the middle of the house, as if they would find safety there. Y'Tin followed the others. When he got there, he found a pregnant woman lying on one of the bedroom floors. Several women were tending to her while a handful of wide-eyed children pressed against a wall. The shaman was leaning over the woman moving his lips.

Y'Tin laid his forehead against a wall. He thought about how his voice had just changed. He knew that was bad and might draw attention to himself, since he might seem more like a man than a boy. And, in fact, right after he had that thought, one of the soldiers started calling for all men twelve and up to separate from the boys. Then Y'Tin spotted Y'Siu and felt that guilty gladness again. They had just exchanged a glance when the screaming for men grew shrill. Y'Tin frowned at the floor, hesitated, and then headed back down the ladder.

It was illogical to send the men up to the longhouse and then call them back outside again. Because it was illogical, Y'Tin knew that anything could happen. These soldiers didn't have to follow orders or rules because nobody was around to enforce rules here in the jungle.

As Y'Siu was still climbing down, a soldier grabbed his arm and jerked him for no reason. Y'Siu lost his balance and fell to the ground. He covered his head with his hands as if to protect himself. "How old are you?" Then, before he could answer, the soldier bellowed again, "How old are you?"

"Fifteen!" Y'Siu cried back. "I'm just fifteen."

The boy soldier appeared again and hog-tied Y'Siu, binding his wrists and ankles. The boy pushed Y'Siu away, barking to another soldier, "Find out what you can from him." He looked at Y'Tin. "What are you staring at?"

Y'Tin reared back in surprise. "Nothing!" he said shrilly. "I wasn't staring at anything!"

A gun fired and Y'Tin whipped around. Y'Siu lay on the ground, his eyes holding an eerie glow, the glow of terror. But he was alive. Y'Tin wondered who had shot the bullet and why.

Then someone knocked Y'Tin's legs from underneath him, sending him sprawling. His thoughts became a series of clicks, as if each moment were separate instead of part of a flowing river.

Click! Live.

Click! Die.

Click! Pain.

Click! Y'Siu.

Click! Fear.

He lay still, unsure whether the soldiers wanted him to stay here or to get up. As rain started to spray down on him, he lay in the mud unmoving, promising the spirits that if he got out of this alive, he would sacrifice a buffalo. But if there were spirits in the village, they were not smiling on Y'Tin.

"Stand up! Stand up!" Y'Tin obeyed instantly, jumping to his feet. The soldiers herded the men toward one of the smaller longhouses. The hard rain grew harder, and Y'Tin doubted that even their captors were having a good time: Everybody was miserable. An old man—Y'Pioc's grandfather— tripped, and Y'Tin braced himself as a soldier raised the butt of his rifle. But nothing happened. The soldier turned away as if he couldn't be bothered with an old man. Y'Tin took a chance and helped Y'Pioc's grandfather to his feet. Luckily, none of the soldiers seemed to care.

But then the boy soldier noticed him again. He knocked Y'Tin's feet out from under him and tied a rope around his ankles. Y'Tin couldn't breathe for a second. He thought he was about to be killed. The boy soldier and another soldier picked up Y'Tin with a grunt and hung him upside down from a ladder at one of the longhouses. Y'Tin had no idea why. Then they left him, the blood flowing to his head until he felt like his scalp was going to explode. He tried to turn his head in different directions so he could see who had been captured. He still hadn't spotted anyone in his family. At least there was that. Then for the first time he realized that if his family wasn't here, that could mean they'd escaped, but it could also mean they were dead. He tried to grab at the rope around his ankles, but somebody whacked his back with something, somehow causing not just his back but his whole body to feel pain.

Y'Tin watched upside down as the soldiers searched longhouse after longhouse for valuables. Every time one of the soldiers passed near Y'Elur, Y'Elur put his palms together and bowed his head and said something. Y'Tin couldn't hear what he was saying. After a while Y'Tin's eyeballs were pulsing from the blood pressure. The soldiers made a pile of valuables: lighters, guns, ammunition, canteens, rice.

The North Vietnamese moved the rest of the men to a different longhouse. Then, again for no reason, someone cut Y'Tin down. He fell straight down on his head and crumpled to the ground. He was hoisted up and thrown under a different longhouse. "Don't move," a soldier snapped.

Y'Tin lay still, his face in the mud, his legs still tied. The rain poured and accumulated in a puddle so that he thought he could actually drown down there. Little by little the water level rose until he realized that he really might drown. He braced himself in case someone was watching, and then he flipped himself onto his back. The rain reached the bottom of his ears. Then a thought filled his head: He was going to die. He fought down that thought and felt viciousness fill his heart. It was as if all his life, a person he didn't know had been residing inside of him, and this person was a killer. He wanted to get free and kill these soldiers.

"Get out of there," a soldier suddenly screamed at him. Y'Tin shimmied out from under the long-house. "Go on, get inside. Get that rope off." With shaking hands, Y'Tin untied the rope from his ankles. He climbed up to the longhouse where the men had been herded. He was surprised at the silence among them. Nobody moved, nobody talked. Y'Tin sat down against a wall. He was still alive.

Chapter Six

The shaman was groaning in a monotone. "Uuuhhhh. Uuuhhhh." Over and over again. Y'Tin spotted Y'Juen and made his way over to him. They walked to the back of the house.

"We'll have to escape," Y'Tin said. "Why separate out the men unless they plan on killing us?"

"Maybe they're taking us to be reeducated."

"Maybe," Y'Tin said, unconvinced.

"Have you noticed the way Y'Elur is trying to get on their good side? I don't trust him."

"Neither do I."

Then Y'Juen nodded almost imperceptibly. Y'Tin turned around and saw Y'Elur making his way to them. When he reached them, he nodded at each. "What are we talking about?" he asked. He put an arm around each of their shoulders. Y'Tin hardly knew Y'Elur. He could not even remember the last time he had spoken to him.

Neither Y'Juen nor Y'Tin answered. Finally, Y'Tin said, "The rain."

"The rain?" Y'Elur repeated.

Y'Tin could kick himself. What a stupid answer. The rain. "Yes, the rain. It's coming down hard now."

"It's pretty wet out there," Y'Juen added.

Y'Elur slapped them both on the shoulders and said, "All right, just wanted to say I'm here if you want to talk about our situation."

Y'Tin didn't even talk to Y'Elur before this whole mess and he certainly wasn't going to talk to him now. But he slapped Y'Elur back on a shoulder and said, "Thanks, Y'Elur."

In a minute he saw Y'Elur slapping someone else on the shoulder. He was turning himself into a spy, no doubt about it.

That first night Y'Tin lay on the floor in one of the rooms beside Y'Juen and a number of other boys. It was cool that night, but the soldiers had taken all the blankets. Y'Tin tried to sleep as the wind whistled through the house.

"What do you think they're going to do with us?" Y'Juen whispered.

Y'Tin didn't answer because he had no answer. The question hung in the air until finally a voice said softly, "They're going to kill us."

"Then why haven't they already done it?" another boy asked.

Y'Tin couldn't stretch out on his back as he usually did because there wasn't enough space. The room was pitch black. He began to wonder how many people had escaped. He guessed that about half of them had been captured, so he hoped the other half had gotten away. If he hadn't come back for Jujubee, he would have escaped with Lady. He hadn't gotten a good look at all the ladies, but as far as he could tell, Jujubee hadn't been captured. But he couldn't get the image of her at the fence out of his mind.

Y'Tin listened to the rain falling. There was a leak in the roof right above him, and they were sleeping so close together, he couldn't move. *Drip. Drip. Drip.* Right on the side of his face. Finally, he couldn't stand it and said, "There's a roof leak on top of me." He felt his way toward the hallway as well as he could. He tripped over someone and thudded against a wall. He felt for where he thought the doorway was, but there was only wall. He maneuvered through the tangle of arms and legs.

"What are you doing?" someone asked with annoyance.

"Trying to get out."

"Who is that—Y'Tin?"

"Yes . . . Y'Elur?"

"Yes, it's me. You're stepping all over everyone."

"Sorry."

Y'Tin finally reached the doorway, where there was another tangle of limbs.

"Who is that? Go to sleep."

"I'm trying," Y'Tin responded. He found a space and squeezed between a body and the wall. He lay wide awake. In fact, he felt as if he had never been so wide awake. "Logically, there's nothing to be gained by killing us," he said to anyone else who was awake.

There was a long silence. Then: "You can't use logic to understand war. Who is that?"

"It's Y'Tin. Who are you?"

"Joseph." Joseph was the shaman. "Have you seen any of my family? I think I saw yours getting away."

"What?" said Y'Tin. "You did?"

"I think so. But it was all happening so fast."

"Did you see Jujubee?"

"No. I saw your parents."

Y'Tin wished he had seen Joseph's family as well, but all he could remember from those early moments was the kick on his nose. He gingerly felt his nose now. It hurt to touch.

His mind began racing. He was scared to sleep. Someone might kill him while he slept. It wasn't logical, but it was possible. Why else had the soldiers herded them all to one place? But he was trying to use logic again. He realized that he heard wailing from a distance. One of the ladies. Then a gunshot sounded, and the wailing stopped. Why were the soldiers holding them here? There was no logic in it. But he had to get this idea of logic out of his head. It would do him no good, and it might do him harm if the soldiers were using emotions. He had to escape. But he couldn't say anything now, with Y'Elur in the next room.

"Go to sleep, Y'Tin," Joseph said.

Y'Tin wondered how the shaman had known he was still awake. He supposed that it was the shaman's job to know everything.

Now that the thought of truly escaping had entered his head, he couldn't get it out. His heart filled with fear over this idea of escape. How would he do it? Would he go by himself? With Y'Juen? If no one would come with him, he would do it alone.

He lay shivering, listening to the rain, wondering how Lady was, wondering how his family was, and wondering when he would finally fall asleep.

Chapter Seven

The soldiers kept the men inside for the next day and night, giving them water but no food. Y'Tin tried not to think too much about escaping in case one of the *m'tao* or *k'sok*—the lower-ranking evil spirits who served the great evil spirit Yang Lie—told the soldiers what he was thinking. Every so often he couldn't resist going to one of the doorways to see what was going on. Tin wondered whether more soldiers were coming. The soldiers all seemed bored. The thought of whether the Rhade lived or died bored them, Y'Tin realized.

On the second night everyone gathered around the shaman.

"I was just a boy when I realized my talents," he was telling them. "I liked to hunt like any young boy. I didn't like farming, but I helped in the fields anyway. People started noticing that my friends never fell ill. They learned that ever since I could talk, I had told my friends what they should sacrifice to keep healthy and prosperous. Then the old shaman trained me in the ways of the stick. He would throw the stick to the ground, and it would shake and bounce though nobody was touching it. I saw this myself." The shaman closed his eyes. "And now our story ends."

Y'Tin thought about this and realized that's what was happening. The North Vietnamese were trying to end the Rhade's story. And they were bored with this ending.

On the third morning Y'Tin heard shouting outside, and he recognized one of the voices as Y'Siu's. He wondered why Y'Siu was outside. Were they interrogating him? The shouting turned to grunts and the grunts turned into a gun firing. Then Y'Siu was quiet. It seemed unreal—almost impossible—that Y'Siu could be dead. Y'Tin rejected the idea. He could not comprehend it.

He walked hesitantly to the front entrance. As

soon as he arrived, the boy soldier looked up at
him. Y'Tin spotted a body lying in the dirt. From
the back, it looked like Y'Siu. It *was* Y'Siu. Blood
dribbled out from under him. The boy smiled
maliciously at Y'Tin. Y'Tin fought back a wave of
nausea and backed inside.

He turned to the men sitting on mats just inside
the longhouse, then closed his eyes and slumped
against the wall. When he opened his eyes, he saw
Y'Siu standing among the men. "Y'Siu!" he cried
out.

"Take care of my elephant for me," Y'Siu
answered calmly.

Y'Tin paused. "But . . ." Y'Tin paused again. He
realized that Y'Siu's body was wavering a bit, as if
from a breeze. Y'Tin stepped forward.

"Take care of Dok," Y'Siu said again, and then
he spread out, the way a cloud spreads out. Then
he was gone.

The men were all looking at Y'Tin with
vague interest. "He's gone," he said, but nobody
answered.

Y'Tin thought, *Why kill a boy who wanted only to
tend to his elephant? And who didn't have any friends
except for me, Tomas, and Dok?*

That night the men could have slept on mats in different rooms, but instead, the men who couldn't fit in the biggest bedroom slept in the hallway so that everyone could sleep close together. Y'Tin kept waking up, and when morning came, he felt as if he hadn't had any sleep at all.

It was barely light out. Y'Juen came up to Y'Tin. "Did you hear the screaming last night?"

Y'Tin shook his head.

"It was awful. She sounded like an animal."

Y'Tin studied the floor and then looked up and said quietly, "I wonder if they missed any guns. Maybe we can find some weapons."

"We'd need a hundred guns to match them," Y'Juen replied.

Y'Tin knew that was true and nodded in agreement. One boy said, "We can't dream of guns where there are none. We need another plan."

Y'Tin didn't know the boy well and didn't say more. He didn't know who he could trust.

"If anyone escapes, they can retrieve the guns from the jungle where our fathers buried them," another boy said.

Y'Tin saw Y'Elur looking over and didn't say more.

For the next few hours the soldiers paid no attention to the captives. Y'Tin grew rather aggressive, sometimes standing on the front porch to see what was going on. But the soldiers were just loitering around, smoking, chewing gum, and occasionally spitting. At mid-morning one of them came up yelling for the men to get outside and line up. They always thought they had to yell. So different from the American Special Forces, who usually talked in calm, measured tones—except when they were playing practical jokes. Y'Tin climbed down with the others.

"Straight line! Make a straight line!" the boy soldier cried. What was the difference? But the men lined up straight. No one had the slightest desire to stand out.

White clouds filled the sky and gave the morning a dreamy, beautiful quality. A crow swept across the village and landed on the slanted roof of the Hlongs' longhouse. Every day that same crow swept across the village and landed on the same roof. Some people thought it was a dead relative of the Hlongs come back as a crow. Y'Tin felt envious of the crow—life was the same as usual to the birds that lived around the village.

An older man joined the boy soldier. They spoke quietly, and the man turned to them.

Y'Tin expected more yelling, but instead, the man spoke so quietly that Y'Tin had to strain to hear. The man looked at Y'Tin. "Your father in FULRO?" FULRO was the United Front for the Liberation of Oppressed Races, whose goal was the independence of the Dega tribes and a separate nation for them in the highlands. His father was indeed a member.

"No," Y'Tin lied.

"What about the Americans? Your father served in Special Forces?"

"No, he's a farmer."

For no reason the soldier turned to a quiet boy who lived across the village from Y'Tin and pushed the barrel of his gun into the boy's ribs. "Come on, to the cemetery. All of you!" At first no one moved, because no good could come of them going to the cemetery. For all Y'Tin knew, he would come to rest there soon, and if that's what the spirits had in mind for him, then so it would be. But if there was any chance to escape, he would. If he had rice wine or a chicken, he would make a sacrifice to the spirits, but he didn't have chicken or wine or anything at all except his loincloth.

At the cemetery Y'Tin looked at the mounds over each of the dead. For those who died of natural causes, the heads of each grave faced east, the way the spirits liked. For all others, the heads faced west. Thirty or forty shovels already lay in a pile on the ground. "Dig," said a soldier. "Come on, dig!" he screamed, before anyone had had a chance to move. Y'Siu's body was lying on the other side of the cemetery. Y'Tin wanted to dig a deep grave for his friend.

He picked up a shovel and rammed it into the earth, digging until his palms were red and oozing with blisters. Unlike the other boys, he never worked in the fields, so he was unaccustomed to digging. By lunchtime they'd dug a hole about three times Y'Tin's height in both length and depth. There could be only one purpose for the hole. He wondered how many people would fit in there. He tried to do the math, but his brain wouldn't work.

In the afternoon the NVA provided them with rice, which the men ate with their fingers like women. Lunch was such a relief that Y'Tin wanted to eat slowly and savor the rice. But he was starving and gobbled his food instead.

Pain ran from Y'Tin's neck down his spine. "I can't keep going," a man named Y'Buom said. Y'Buom was known for complaining; still, Y'Tin couldn't stop a short, surprised gasp over someone daring to talk. But no one hit Y'Buom and no one shot him. Y'Tin didn't know if that was good or bad.

Y'Buom stood up and repeated to one of the soldiers, "I can't go on."

Two guns fired almost simultaneously, and Y'Buom fell to the ground. A stocky soldier put him over his shoulder and walked to the other end of the cemetery to throw him on top of Y'Siu. Y'Tin looked into his rice bowl and tried to keep his hands from shaking.

One of the older soldiers told them quietly, "Go on, back to work." Y'Tin's back and palms started to hurt so much that all this digging became a form of torture. He tried to separate his three spirits from his body, so that he wouldn't feel the pain. But it didn't work. His hands hurt and his back hurt, and he kept going anyway. He did not want to get shot down and thrown over his friend Y'Siu.

The hole was now about four times Y'Tin's height square and still three times his height deep. The soldiers gave no sign that the workday might be ending. The bigger the hole got, the more people they planned on killing. Y'Tin wondered whether he was helping to dig the grave for what was left of the villagers. If he died, he hoped Tomas would keep his word and take care of Lady.

It was only when it started getting dark that one of the soldiers finally said, "That's enough, get back to the longhouse."

The men didn't get more rice for dinner, but Y'Tin was grateful for the water they received. "I hope they kill me first," a man said. "I don't want to have to go last." Nobody answered him. Y'Tin didn't want to go first *or* last. He wanted to escape . . . but he was so tired.

When Y'Tin lay down to sleep later, his palms were crusted with dried blood. His hands were like useless claws. That was his last thought before sleeping. His first thought upon waking was fear— he thought the soldiers were shaking him awake because he was next to die. It was too dark to see who had awakened him. Then Y'Juen whispered, "Y'Tin. Y'Tin. Get up."

"What is it?" Y'Tin whispered back. He sat up. His back ached when he moved.

"One of the old men just died. Y'Siu's great-grandfather."

Y'Tin followed Y'Juen to where an oil lamp

illuminated a small crowd standing around the dead man. He peeked out the side door and saw that it was unguarded. Then he went to the front door and saw the two guards talking to each other.

He reported to Y'Juen, "The guard at the side door is gone. He's in front talking."

"What?"

"Shhh!"

"Do you think we could get out?" Y'Juen said softly.

"Yes."

"If we stay here, we're safer," Y'Juen pointed out. "If they were going to kill us all, they would have done it today after the hole was finished."

Y'Tin said, "Maybe the hole isn't finished." Y'Tin looked at the dead man. The dim room suddenly seemed liquid, flowing around him. Y'Tin tried to make it all stay still, but he was so scared. "I'm going," he whispered. "Are you coming or staying?"

"I guess I'm coming. Right now?" Y'Juen asked.

"What do you mean, you 'guess'?"

"Yes, I'm coming with you."

They tried to look through the rooms for anything useful they could find, but the dim light made their search futile. They slipped down the long corridor, and at the side door Y'Tin saw that the guard was still gone.

Y'Tin wanted to tell others about the unguarded door, but he was afraid that Y'Elur would report them. He poked his head out the doorway and looked around. He saw nobody. As he climbed down, a sense of vertigo suddenly made the world spin, and he stumbled down the last step. He lay on his stomach and didn't move. He felt a drop on his arm and for a moment thought one of the soldiers was playing with them, somehow sending drops their way to torment them. Another drop fell, and Y'Tin noticed the sky was gray with clouds.

Y'Tin wriggled forward, Y'Juen following. Y'Tin heard shouting and cringed, but the shouting had nothing to do with them. Unfortunately, the men were being held in a longhouse far from the gate. Y'Tin did not think they could crawl all the way out and not be seen. There were too many North Vietnamese for that.

They crawled along, and a few longhouses down he turned to Y'Juen and gestured toward one of them. They climbed the ladder and sat for a second in the darkened hallway. "We can stay here until they leave," Y'Tin whispered. Y'Tin's mouth didn't seem to be working right. He could barely enunciate the words. And his hands were shaking.

They crept to a middle bedroom and lay silent, listening. Y'Tin suddenly wanted to cry, but he didn't because he was afraid it might make noise. He was wide awake. He hoped Y'Elur didn't notice they were gone and report them. Y'Tin prayed to Ai Die, Yang Lie, and even to Y'Siu. After all, they would need as much help as they could get. Y'Tin couldn't fall asleep and lay for hours staring into the darkness, listening for any sound that might mean they'd been discovered. He felt strangely powerful, felt he would hear a whisper even if it occurred across the village. That's how hard he was listening.

He must have fallen asleep because he woke to find Y'Juen sitting with his back pressed against a wall, as if the wall were all that was holding him up. Y'Juen came over and whispered, "I thought you were sick—it's so late. There's half a bucket of water in the front kitchen."

Y'Tin nodded gratefully and went to the kitchen to find the bucket. He drank only as much as he had to, even though his mouth was so dry that his tongue stuck to his lips.

Afterward he and Y'Juen searched from room to room looking for anything of value that soldiers had missed. They found one lighter, two crossbows with four arrows, three American canteens, one American military poncho, and a couple of brightly colored woven bags. Y'Tin thought of his own colorful bag, atop Lady the last time he had seen it. He longed to be lying on her back. Once, when he was sick, he had gotten out of his sickbed in the longhouse and staggered over to Lady, climbing up her back to lie there. He fell asleep, and when he awoke, evening had fallen and Lady hadn't moved. It was as if she knew he was sleeping and needed her to be still so he wouldn't tumble off.

After their search Y'Tin and Y'Juen sat against a wall. Neither of them spoke for hours, and they moved only when one part of their body grew sore. Then they heard popping noises, over and over, but they didn't risk peeking out the doorways. Y'Tin stared at the wood floor and groaned softly. When the popping ended, he thought angrily of Y'Elur. He wondered whether his duplicity had paid off and the soldiers had allowed him to live. Y'Tin would not want to live if he had betrayed his own people.

They hid in the longhouse for three days. Y'Tin's head grew woozy from fear and lack of food. Sometimes he saw stars when he moved suddenly. And then after a while Y'Tin felt bored. How was it possible to be bored at such a time? And yet he was. He'd never been cooped inside for three days in his whole life.

On the third night he and Y'Juen fell asleep, and Y'Tin awoke to a crackling sound and the smell of smoke. The crackling was all around them. He was immediately wide awake—the house was on fire! "Y'Juen! Wake up!" Y'Juen opened his eyes. "The house is on fire. We have to go!" Y'Tin cried. Then he said what his father had said: "Now. We have to go *now*."

They grabbed their bags and jumped off the front porch. A single soldier stood at the east end of the pathway through the village, but Y'Tin didn't see anyone else. "Hey!" the soldier called out to them. "Stop or I'll shoot!"

Y'Tin and Y'Juen ran through the village, hearing gunshots behind them. Neither of them broke stride. They spotted another soldier running through the gate, and without speaking or signaling, both veered south, where the houses were closer together. They scrambled up into a house and didn't move.

The soldiers were shouting to one another, but Y'Tin couldn't hear what they were saying. They seemed to be several houses away. Y'Tin and Y'Juen looked at each other, and then they both moved toward the side entrance of the house. They climbed down the ladder and went south, where they spotted a gap in the burning fence.

The night was intensely bright, but a strange, red-hued bright, making the night eerie and bizarre. The crackling sounded all around them. The burning seemed random. One house would be nearly burned to the ground and another would be totally intact. Y'Tin heard the flames blowing in the wind—it sounded like the wind rippling a blanket his mother had hung on their clothesline.

They crept along the ground, just in case there were soldiers they had missed. It seemed to take forever to reach the fence, and they knew that somewhere behind them the soldiers were searching. When they finally reached the fence, relief flooded Y'Tin's heart. Despite the embers, Y'Tin and Y'Juen crawled through the gap. Y'Tin felt the embers burning his skin, but he didn't stop.

On the other side of the fence the fields were empty in the eerie glow from the fire. Y'Tin stood up and ran as fast as he could, and he knew without looking that Y'Juen was also running. They headed straight for the jungle, and when they reached it, they plunged into the trees.

It was too dark to see. They moved slowly. Y'Tin heard the crack of a twig he must have broken as he walked forward. He froze for a moment, but it seemed there was nobody to hear the crack. He realized that if someone searched for them in the morning, there would be all sorts of broken twigs and disturbances that would make it easy to see their trail. He doubted anyone would follow them tomorrow, because two boys didn't mean a thing in this war. But tonight—that was something else. The soldiers had nothing better to do tonight but search for a couple of boys. The important thing to do at the moment was to get some distance between the village and themselves.

Before taking another step, however, Y'Tin peered toward his village. He couldn't see anything through the leaves. But he didn't need to see the village to know suddenly that everybody who'd been captured was now dead. Even Y'Elur. Even the shy girl.

He turned around then, and he and Y'Juen moved as fast as they could as quietly as they could. But they were making enough noise to be followed if anybody desired to do so. Y'Tin had never rushed like this from anything before. He had only rushed toward something—usually the village or the elephants. It was weird, the way even in this emergency he had time to think as they thrashed through the jungle, away from their village. Or not "their" village. They had no village now. The only place for them now was here in the jungle.

Y'Juen suddenly stopped, causing Y'Tin to fall into him.

"What is it?" Y'Tin asked.

"We should cover our trail, or they'll be able to find us in the morning. I'll do it."

"It's too dark now to even see our trail!" Y'Tin said.

Y'Juen didn't reply at first. Then he said testily, "Who put you in charge?" Since he was older, Y'Juen had always been the leader of the two of them. But as Y'Tin's father liked to say, different situations called for different leaders.

"We need to put distance between ourselves and the village," Y'Tin snapped. He couldn't even remember the last time he had snapped at Y'Juen. Maybe he had never done so.

This time Y'Juen didn't answer at all. They continued quietly through the jungle until Y'Tin finally said, "Do you know what direction we're going in?"

"West?" Y'Juen said. "North?"

"We could be going in a circle!"

They decided to stop and rest for the remainder of the night. They slept under the U.S. Army poncho. Everywhere you turned, signs of the Americans popped up. That was the weird thing about them. Even here, though the Americans had abandoned the Rhade, Y'Tin and Y'Juen slept under one of their ponchos. The fact was, once the Rhade had fought with the Americans, their spirits were joined. The Rhade had trusted the Americans. And this was where it had led them.

In the morning Y'Tin woke up second again. Y'Juen was eating coconut. He offered a piece to Y'Tin, who gobbled it up. He'd never particularly liked coconut, but now it tasted as good as a chicken. "I found elephant tracks," Y'Juen said. "It might be Lady and the others."

"What? Where?"

Y'Juen's mouth was full, but he gestured with his hand. Y'Tin got up and walked in the direction Y'Juen had gestured toward. Sure enough, there were three distinct elephant trails, as well as one human trail. His heart lifted as he saw that a couple of the elephant prints were almost perfectly circular. Those belonged to Geng. Y'Tin had noticed the perfect circles of her tracks before. She had stepped onto a bare, muddy patch of dirt and laid down two perfect prints. Y'Tin studied the succulent plants covering much of the ground and saw many breaks and disturbances.

"Do you think it's them?" Y'Juen whispered.

"Absolutely," he said, using the word the Americans had loved. Then he switched back to speaking Rhade again. "The elephants have to stop a lot to eat, so we'll catch up soon." He spoke softly, for even though it was unlikely anybody was around, you couldn't be too cautious. They made a point of not talking unless it was utterly necessary.

They continued until thirst stopped them. They cut open a couple of bamboo stalks and drank the water from inside. The air smelled sweet, and the smell turned out to be overripe bananas. Y'Tin was famished, and mushy bananas seemed like a feast.

CYNTHIA KADOHATA

Late that afternoon the trail was so fresh that Y'Tin started running forward in excitement. The trail was easy to make out now. He didn't even glance at it anymore, just ran forward in the general direction of the tracks. About twenty minutes later Y'Tin and Y'Juen came upon the elephants feeding with Tomas. Y'Tin ran right toward Lady. When Lady spotted him, she trotted over, picked him up with her trunk, threw him to the ground, and bonked him on the head. Then her trunk swayed back and forth the way it did when she was happy. Y'Tin tried to stay calm so she wouldn't pick him up and throw him down again. He stood still while she stroked her trunk this way and that over his face.

"Y'Tin, you're safe!" Tomas was crying out. He pulled Y'Tin away from Lady and grabbed him with both arms. "You're safe! Where are the others? Did everyone get out in time?"

There was much to say, but Y'Tin couldn't think. "Tomas . . ."

When Y'Tin didn't say more, Tomas turned to Y'Juen and slapped his shoulder. "Glad to see you." He turned immediately back to Y'Tin and grabbed his shoulders again. "And Y'Siu?"

All of a sudden, Y'Tin's elation evaporated.

"The soldiers killed him," he told Tomas. "I saw his body." He gulped. "I saw his ghost."

Tomas's arms dropped. "Y'Siu? *Y'Siu?* Why would anyone kill Y'Siu?" He shook his head as though to shake the very idea out of his brain. After a moment, though, he asked, "Did he have a proper burial?"

"There was a mass grave." Y'Tin held back a sob.

Tomas shook his head over and over again. Y'Tin felt dizzy. He motioned Lady to *muk* so he could climb on her back. As he lay across her, he felt as if she were replenishing his energy supply.

"A mass grave?" Tomas said. "Are you sure? Did you see the grave?"

"I helped dig it," Y'Tin replied.

"What!"

"All the men did. They brought us to the cemetery and made us dig a hole."

"For everyone? Our whole village?"

"Some of them seem to have gotten away. Lots. Maybe half," Y'Juen answered.

"And . . . and my family? Did you see them?"

"None of them," Y'Tin replied.

Y'Tin watched Tomas soak in this detail. He seemed confused, unsure whether the news was good or bad. Then he said, "That's good."

Y'Tin continued to lie atop Lady. Tomas and Y'Juen took the other elephants to a nearby river. When Y'Tin felt stronger, he slipped down Lady's side and said, "Lady, *nao*." He headed in the same direction as his friends.

When Y'Tin and Lady reached the river, Y'Juen and Tomas were down the way, watching the elephants drink. Y'Tin wanted to be alone right now, so he didn't go stand with them. Lady filled her trunk and sprayed it into her mouth, over and over.

"Y'Tin!" shouted Tomas. Y'Tin waved at Tomas. Tomas continued. "Go back to camp and get our things. Hurry, we need to get going."

It wasn't that far back to camp, but Tomas's tone annoyed Y'Tin. Tomas hadn't talked to him that way since Y'Tin was in training. And he couldn't believe that Tomas was yelling when they all should be quieter than that. Maybe Tomas didn't understand how bad things were right now. He'd been isolated in the jungle with the elephants. So Y'Tin shrugged off Tomas's yelling and returned to camp. He knew which things were his and Y'Juen's. Everything else he put in Tomas's bag.

When he returned, Tomas took his bag and declared that they'd head west. "We need to put distance between us and the soldiers and then decide what to do," he said. "Y'Tin, carry my bag. I need to concentrate."

Y'Tin didn't see why Tomas couldn't carry his bag and concentrate at the same time, and he also didn't see why Tomas didn't just hang his bag around Geng's neck.

The elephants lumbered through the jungle, their padded feet absorbing the noise of their footfalls. A bird called out—*cawww! cawww!*—from high atop a tree. Somewhere a monkey howled. Y'Tin spotted a bright green bamboo pit viper, and his pulse raced. He remembered that Shepard called the snake a "two-stepper" because when you got bit by one, you'd be dead in two steps. Y'Tin kept his distance.

It felt as if they were making little progress because the elephants kept stopping to feed. It seemed they spent most of their waking hours eating and drinking or wishing they were eating and drinking.

At first they traveled silently, Y'Tin's mind racing about where they were going and where they were coming from. He thought his family would likely be heading west as well and for the same reason. Y'Tin knew that at some point one of them would have to find out for certain what had happened at the village and also where the villagers who had escaped were. But for now they needed to operate in panic mode. One thing his father said was that panic could be controlled and used. Supposedly, when you were panicked, you didn't notice how hungry you were. Since Y'Tin felt ravenous for some meat, he figured he wasn't panicked anymore.

The next time the elephants stopped, the boys watched as the animals examined the possibilities. Their trunks moved here and there, as the elephants decided what they should eat. Lady tore at some grass, and after she'd made a pile of it, she pushed it this way and that. Finally, she picked some up and placed it into her mouth. Y'Tin was starving. He wished he could eat grass.

"Should we go hunting?" Y'Tin asked. "I'm hungry."

"Eat another banana," Tomas replied.

An irrational anger surged in Y'Tin's chest. He wanted meat. He did not want another banana. When his mother had meatless days, Y'Tin often dreamed that night of meat. Now it was all he could think of.

Y'Juen was patting Dok's hide and murmuring

to her. Dok took a few steps away and stood there. She was missing Y'Siu. But Y'Tin's mind was on meat. He wished that he and Y'Juen had had an opportunity to search the village for chickens. His mouth salivated as he thought of cooked chicken. He pulled a banana out of his bag and peeled it unenthusiastically.

Tomas gave Y'Tin a sharp look. "At least we're not starving. Don't complain."

"I didn't say anything."

"You were thinking something, though."

"So now I'm not supposed to think?" retorted Y'Tin.

Tomas closed his eyes and took a big breath. Then he turned away from Y'Tin as if he couldn't waste any more time on him.

After the elephants ate their fill, the boys climbed up on them to ride. The jungle grew darker and darker. When Y'Tin could hardly see, Tomas said, "We'll stop now." They slid off the elephants. Y'Tin was still annoyed that Tomas hadn't wanted to go hunting. Now all Y'Tin would dream about as he slept was meat. Tomas laid a hand on his shoulder. Y'Tin thought that was an apology until Tomas said, "We were thinking you should go back to scout tomorrow and see what happened to the people who were captured."

"Me?"

"You're such a good tracker," Tomas said, slapping his shoulder. "We really admire that about you. With your tracking skills, you'll be the safest."

So Y'Tin was elected.

The boys lay on the jungle floor. Y'Tin spread the poncho over himself and Y'Juen. The ground was cold against Y'Tin's bare back. If he'd had more time, he would have brought one of the shirts his father had bought in Ban Me Thuot.

"My father once said that guerillas need half a day to fight or travel and half a day to hunt for food," said Y'Tin. And, of course, if his father said so, it was true. But Y'Tin did not say more, sensing that Tomas might take offense at suggestions that weren't asked for. Y'Tin was too tired for another quarrel. He remembered that a few years ago some boys from the village had gotten lost in the jungle. When they finally returned home, they mentioned that they had squabbled almost constantly with one another. At the time his father had said to Y'Tin, "The jungle changes a man." But even knowing this did not make Y'Tin feel less mad.

Far away, gunfire sounded. It went on and on. "It's a battle," said Tomas.

Y'Juen asked, "Do you think it's our village?"

Tomas paused. Then: "No, it's coming from another direction."

Lady slept a few meters away. She'd been subdued all day, and Y'Tin wondered if her pregnancy was making her tired. In the dim light he could see her stomach bulging. She looked as if she could give birth at any moment. He closed his eyes but still felt wide awake. He knew he must sleep to be strong for whatever might come next. He wondered whether his father was fighting somewhere at that very moment.

Y'Tin did not even know if his mother had changed her mind about leaving the village at the last minute. He did not know if that was really Jujubee he had seen near the fence. He did not know how his aunts and uncles had fared. He felt a pain inside. He opened his eyes. He had to know what had become of everyone. He felt glad that he was the one who would go back to the village. He wanted to see it for himself. But he was annoyed that neither Tomas nor Y'Juen had talked to him before they decided. Y'Tin wondered vaguely when they had decided this. When had they become a "we"?

Chapter Eight

W hen Y'Tin awoke, his face was damp
with dew. He felt something on his
elbow and saw a centipede as long
as his forearm. "Ah!" he cried. He jumped up and
shook the insect off. Jujubee was allergic to centipede venom and had once gotten sick for a week
after being bitten. Y'Juen had shoes, so he stamped
it to death.

"Thanks," Y'Tin said.

Tomas was also awake, brushing Geng. Geng
loved being brushed, and Tomas tried to brush her
several times a day. He looked Y'Tin's way and said,
"You'd better get started."

Y'Tin laid his forehead against Lady's trunk and

thought, *Good-bye. I'll be back.* Then he slipped away on his mission. He was so nervous, his ears filled with pounding. He could hardly hear anything else. The pounding seemed to shake his whole body. He stood still and concentrated on silencing the pounding before setting off again.

He put the danger out of his mind as he glided forward. He swam across the river and traveled through heavy bush, the plants scraping against his bare arms. Later, when he reached the halfway point to his village, he could feel something ominous in the air. He stood still, listening.

Then he noticed human footprints in the moss. They were fresh and perpendicular to Y'Tin's direction. A bug squirmed in one of them, meaning the print was so fresh that the squashed bug hadn't even died yet. Y'Tin told himself to stay calm. The tracks were fresh, but they were going in a different direction. Then he heard voices. He froze. The pounding sound in his ears grew so loud, he couldn't hear the voices anymore. But he knew the voices were there. There was such a din in his ears that for a moment he thought he was losing his mind. He fought the instinct to crouch lower. Instead, he stayed as still as possible. He thought to himself over and over, *I won't die. It's my destiny to take care of Lady. I won't die. It's my destiny to take care of Lady.* The spirits were not with him— another centipede crawled over his foot. He closed his eyes and concentrated on staying still as the centipede paused on his ankle and then didn't stir, as if it had fallen asleep. After about a half an hour, the centipede began crawling up his leg, and Y'Tin couldn't stop himself from brushing it off.

It was growing dark when he dared move again. He hadn't moved before that because he wasn't sure what he did or didn't hear. He decided to set off again.

The closer Y'Tin got to his village, the more certain he was of where he was going. He knew where he was by feeling the trees. He had spent countless hours in this part of the jungle, and he knew the trees almost as well as if he could see them. At the same time the area also felt strange, even new. He felt as if he had been gone for months.

There were no signs of people as he slipped through the gate. For a moment he stood amazed. Nearly every house had been touched by fire. He had once walked through a section of jungle that had been bombed. The carcasses of two elephants and a monkey had lain on the ground, their flesh torn open. The village looked as if a bomb had hit it, and the houses looked like carcasses. All that was left of some of them were the stilts. Other houses were nearly intact. Others had lost only their roofs. Others were gone completely. The soldiers had taken the time to set every house on fire. Why did the soldiers hate them so much? Then his own heart filled with hatred. He had always been fascinated by the missions his father had gone on, but that was just because he was drawn to the adventure of it. This—right now—was the first time he really understood what his father had been fighting for with the Americans.

He watched a few last embers twinkle in the darkness. For the first time in his life, Y'Tin questioned the spirits—after all, what did it matter which spirit had burned these houses? If it was Yang Lie, so what? If it wasn't Yang Lie, so what again? He walked to where his house had been. Dead chickens lay in what had been the chicken coop. The chickens had burned to death. There were large empty rice-wine jars all over the place. Maybe burning a village was easier if you were drunk. And maybe killing people was easier if you were drunk.

Y'Tin knew where he had to go next. He knew the people who had been captured were buried in the cemetery, but he had to make absolutely certain. He did not want to see the cemetery, but he had to. He walked through the gate and stepped along the edge of the jungle until he reached the cemetery. The large hole had been expanded far wider than it was before, and it was all filled in with dirt. He had no way of knowing how deep it was now. He stared a second. Then he dug at the dirt with his hands. He didn't have to dig deep—only about a third of a meter. Then he accidentally touched someone's skin and pulled his hand away with a shout. But he couldn't stop himself from looking at what he had touched: It looked like an ear. He quickly swept the dirt back into place. It was too much; he couldn't comprehend it. He suddenly felt faint and lay down on top of the hole, hugging his knees to his chest.

When Y'Tin had seen the bombed-out area of the jungle, he had thought, *Why drop a bomb? What sense did it make?* Now he wanted to drop a bomb on the soldiers who had killed two hundred and fifty people, who had burned his village and probably other villages as well. And he wanted to talk to these soldiers. He wanted to ask them, *How does it feel? The village is decimated—how does that feel? Two hundred and fifty people are lying in the dirt—how does that feel?* Y'Tin was curious to hear the answers to these questions.

Y'Tin didn't like being this angry. He felt as if his heart was previously clean and now it was dirty with hatred. He wanted to see Lady, to lie on her back and cleanse his heart.

Rain began to fall heavily, but he still didn't move, just stared ahead. He didn't know how much time elapsed before he could finally stand up again. He wiped the water from his face.

Someone called out to him, "Hey! Hey!" His heart seemed to stop, and he ran back into the jungle, terrified. The voice called again. "Say! You are Rhade?"

Y'Tin took a second to decide whether to reply. The man seemed to have a fine Rhade accent. "I am Rhade," he answered loudly.

"I'm from Ban Me Thuot."

The man stood in the shadows near the remnants of the fence. He was very tall, taller even than the village shaman had been. Also, he was dressed like a soldier.

"Step forward," Y'Tin demanded.

"You first. You're just a boy, aren't you?"

"Why are you here if you're from Ban Me Thuot?"

"The town was overrun. The war is nearly over."

Y'Tin didn't trust the man and galloped into the jungle.

"Wait! Where are you going? Come back! I'm all alone!"

The bushes behind Y'Tin thrashed. Y'Tin ran faster, pushing through the jungle as branches scraped his face. He started to wonder whether it was a spirit and not a man at all who was chasing him. The man didn't seem to be losing ground, though Y'Tin moved swiftly. Maybe the man was one of the spirits of the dead. "Ah," Y'Tin groaned as a branch snapped into his left eye. He fell down, tripping over his feet. His eye was closed. He knew it was bleeding but couldn't worry about it now. He shook off a fear that he would die—here, tonight.

"Ahhhh," the man groaned. Y'Tin thought he heard him thump down, and he felt satisfied that the man was also in pain. His intuition told him the man wasn't from Ban Me Thuot. Both Shepard and Y'Tin's father had told him that it was important to use intuition in a war. Anyway, it must have been a man, because a spirit would have caught him by now. After a moment the movement behind Y'Tin stopped, then started again. This time the movement was going away from him, not toward him.

Y'Tin began creeping forward, using his hands to guard his eyes from another branch. He concentrated on not making a single sound. He moved his feet so gently forward that he could not even hear the crunch of leaves. He passed a coconut tree on an odd angle. He knew that tree. The reason it was at an odd angle was that Lady had almost pulled it down once to get a coconut. Sometimes he thought Lady pulled down trees just to see Y'Tin scramble out of the way.

He listened for the man but could not hear a sound. If someone was behind him, that person was a master of staying quiet. Y'Tin crept forward. He liked to think he was a master of staying quiet himself.

As Y'Tin reached less familiar territory, he had no sense of where he was. Every so often a touch of moonlight seemed to flicker in his vision. But he didn't know whether the light was in his imagination. He didn't think of himself as having a lot of imagination, so he decided that the moonlight was real. Then a gun fired somewhere behind him, and he wondered if someone had died.

Y'Tin kept his hands in front of his face and felt the ground with his feet before he stepped forward. A vine hit his face, and he almost cried out. Step by slow step, he moved farther and farther from the village. Once, he felt so overcome with stress that he had to sit down for a few minutes. For no reason his heart suddenly beat as hard as if he were running. He sat on the cold, dark jungle floor. Because he was losing his sense of direction, he did not think he should go on; on the other hand he did not think he should stay here. Then slowly, he felt better—not good, but better. He pulled himself up and continued in what he thought was the direction away from his village.

Even though he was getting exhausted, he didn't stop. Then he lost all sense of direction and finally fell to the ground with no idea where he was. The soles of his feet—as hard as wood—felt tender. He did not understand why it had come to this. He did not understand why his people had been cursed. It wasn't possible that all of the Rhade people had offended the spirits. Maybe the shaman had been right and it was simply time for the Rhade story to end.

Y'Tin lay down on the mossy jungle floor. He hadn't brought the poncho because it rustled too much when you moved. Lying there, without cover, he felt completely alone for the first time in his life. Half of his village was dead. *Half of his village was dead.* He shivered, partly because he was cold and partly because he was afraid. He wondered if he would ever feel safe again or if safety was gone from his life forever.

He felt pebbles under his back and pushed them away, but underneath them lay more pebbles. He turned on his side and pulled his legs against his chest. That felt better, warmer. Trying to make himself smaller, he pushed his face toward his bent knees. He missed Lady.

A branch cracked and he stopped breathing. Something rustled the leaves and then headed away from Y'Tin. He let out his breath. He hoped he would live through the night.

The next morning he woke up before sunrise. The green shades of the jungle seemed gray in the dim light. A million shades of gray, just like the hide of an elephant. His heart filled with relief that he had made it through the night. He closed his eyes and thanked Ai Die for letting him live and prayed that he would die of old age. Then he added that he hoped Lady would die of old age as well. Usually, elephants died by starvation because they grew only six sets of teeth during their lives. When their last pair wore down, the elephants starved. He had promised Lady that he would mash her food when her teeth gave out. After that thought, he amended his prayer once again by adding that he hoped his whole family would die of old age. Then he wanted to pray for his aunts and uncles, but he didn't because he didn't want to annoy Ai Die by asking for too much. He would pray for them later.

With the sun, his sense of direction kicked in and he set off. As he neared the spot where he'd last seen Tomas and Y'Juen, his heart beat faster. But when he got there, the camp was empty. Panic rose in his chest and he waited until it subsided. His mind shut off and then, eventually, turned back on again. He thought about the possibilities and decided there were only two. Either he had come to the right spot or he had not. He scanned the ground, looking for footprints, and felt panic rising again. Then he found a place where the elephants had mashed down the grass. He squatted down. The footprints were covered over, as if Tomas and Y'Juen had hastily tried to hide their trail. But trackers who weren't particularly talented disturbed the environment so much that trying to hide their trail actually made it easier to follow them. Y'Tin knew that. You just had to know how to look. He jumped up, caught sight of the direction they'd headed in, and broke into a trot.

Now that he saw it, the trail was easy to follow. The tracks ended a couple of kilometers away at the river. Y'Tin crossed to the other side, pausing to drink some of the water. But at the other side he could not pick up the trail. Stupid mistake: They had not crossed as he'd thought but had merely walked in the water, probably to hide their footprints. He crossed back to the other side and searched for the trail. Nothing.

Once more Y'Tin crossed the river, panic returning even stronger than before. He tried to pick up the trail farther down from where he'd looked before. When he still couldn't find it, he needed to tell himself to stay calm.

Finally, he searched in the only place he had

not: across the river, north of where he'd searched before. And sure enough, he picked up the trail. He'd wasted about two hours searching. He broke into a jog until the tracks grew fresher and fresher. They were simple to follow now. Y'Juen and Tomas had broken a new trail in deep jungle and, eventually, had returned to the river. Y'Tin trotted along the riverbank. His father would be proud of him, the way he was using his panic. Then he heard elephant trumpeting and raced toward the sound. But when he reached a small clearing, he stopped short. Instead of Lady, Geng, and Dok, twelve elephants—eight cows and four calves, including an infant—were feeding under a patch of blue sky. He'd seen a wild herd only a couple of times before. The other two times, he'd climbed a tree and just watched them, soaking in their beauty.

The twelve elephants stopped eating at the sight of Y'Tin. At first they just stared, and then, agitated, they began moving back and forth on their feet, their ears fanned out. Suddenly, Dok appeared. She walked forward, and the wild elephants grew even more agitated. The biggest one looked like she was going to charge. Y'Tin called out, "Come back! Dok!" She looked at him but did not budge. She would have listened to Y'Siu. In fact, Y'Tin had never seen her not come when called. Then he spotted Lady at the edge of the clearing. She was watching with fascination. He wished he had his hook with him.

The largest cow snorted into the air. "Dok!" Y'Tin called out again. Dok looked at him, hesitated, and then turned her back to him. The largest cow took a couple of steps forward. Lady also took a couple of steps forward. "Lady!" Y'Tin called crisply. She looked at him, and then she and Dok turned their attention back to the wild elephants. Dok's ears flared out, as they always did when she was upset.

A moment later Y'Juen and Tomas appeared. Y'Juen poked at Dok with a hook. "Dok!" Dok slowly turned to him. She looked angry, and for a moment Y'Tin thought she was going to rush Y'Juen. She raised her trunk in the air and trumpeted.

"Lady!" cried Y'Tin. "Come! Come!" She swayed from foot to foot, and then, to his great relief, she finally stepped away from the elephant herd. Dok also joined Y'Tin and Y'Juen. As they all carefully walked away, Y'Tin looked back toward the large cow. She hadn't returned to her herd, but a couple of the other elephants were already starting to eat again.

With the wild elephants out of sight, Lady knocked Y'Tin down with her trunk. He laughed and got up. To his ears, his laugh sounded almost hysterical, so eager was he to be laughing.

"Did you have trouble finding us?" asked Tomas.

"It put me off for a few minutes," Y'Tin lied coolly. He waited to see what Tomas would say next.

"We saw fresh human tracks close by and decided we should leave. What did you find out about the village?"

Y'Tin paused. How could he possibly explain what he'd seen? "I saw the hole in the cemetery. It was filled in. I don't know how many . . . the hole was big," Y'Tin said. He couldn't bear to talk about the people who'd been killed—all he could talk about was the hole. "The hole was bigger than when I saw it the last time. And some of the long-houses are burned to the ground. Most of them. Some of the fence is burned. My home is gone." He needed to stop for a moment as his voice caught. "Yours was half gone, Tomas." He hadn't seen Y'Juen's house because it was on the far side of the village. "I saw the hole," Y'Tin said for the second time. "It seemed big enough . . . it seemed big." He saw Tomas's throat move, as if he had gulped.

"Maybe they took prisoners," Y'Juen said hopefully.

"I hope so," Y'Tin said. That was the best they could wish for, but somehow he knew in his heart that the North Vietnamese had taken no prisoners. Sadness weighted him down, a sadness so heavy he couldn't stay standing. He lay down on the ground.

"You didn't find out anything for a fact!" Y'Juen said. "I already knew as much as you."

"We should have gone ourselves," Tomas said, shaking his head.

Y'Tin didn't want to believe what he'd seen either. Tomas and Y'Juen could resist him if they wanted, but that would not change the truth. "I dug into the hole and felt an ear and then filled the hole again. Ai Die would not like me digging up the dead that way." He stayed on the ground until Lady sniffed at him with her trunk. She wanted a scratch.

As Y'Tin scratched Lady with her brush, Tomas and Y'Juen set up a spit. They'd caught a crow, a good catch because birds were hard to get.

Although you could hear them, you often couldn't see them because they were hiding in the trees. Tomas used bits of dry grass for kindling and dead branches for the fire, then picked thirty bamboo shoots and arranged them in a circle. That was Y'Juen's idea.

Then Tomas began to chant:

"We have almost nothing
We beg the spirits
To show us mercy
To give us luck hunting
The spirits are so powerful
And we are so meek
We, uh, we hope for meat
We beg for luck hunting
For the spirits are so powerful
And we are so meek."

Chapter Nine

When they had finished eating the crow and some bananas, Y'Tin said, "I was worried we might see an elephant fight."

Tomas paused before replying, "I was too. I've never seen Lady interested in other elephants before."

"Neither have I," Y'Tin agreed. Lady had never been overly friendly with elephants—she was almost aloof with Geng and Dok.

"We're lucky we've run into only one herd," Tomas said "I hope there aren't any others in the area. We have enough to worry about." Tomas and Y'Juen glanced at each other and then Tomas added, "We were talking about some things." Y'Tin waited in silence. Tomas glanced at Y'Juen again and went on. "We were just wondering about your attitude, Y'Tin. We need to try harder to get along."

That "we" again. It really bothered Y'Tin. Still, what was the harm if they were a "we" now? After all, he had always forgiven Y'Juen when he ran after the older boys. Y'Juen's insecurity wasn't his fault. His heart was good. But his father was always very, very hard on him, and it had weakened him rather than strengthening him.

Y'Tin thought again of the village boys who had gotten lost in the jungle and had bickered the whole time—how his father had said that was because the jungle changes a man. Y'Tin decided this was why he wasn't getting along with Y'Juen and Tomas. But that didn't explain why the two of them had turned on *him*. And then Y'Juen said, "Yes, Y'Tin, your attitude isn't helping matters any."

Y'Tin's anger level soared sky-high. *His* attitude was fine. It was Y'Juen's and Tomas's fault that they weren't all getting along. Y'Tin decided that Y'Juen did not have such a good heart after all.

"Yes, we think you've been acting a bit different than we're used to," Tomas said. "We all need to work together now." Then, out of nowhere, Tomas said to

Y'Tin, "We wouldn't be in this situation if . . ."

"If what?"

"If it weren't for you."

"What do you mean by that?" Y'Tin asked, jumping up.

"Your father worked for the Special Forces. You even went on a mission once."

"Lots of men worked with the Americans," Y'Tin retorted. He squeezed his hands into fists as hard as he could—that helped contain his anger.

"They brought danger. You said half the village is dead. If that's true, whose fault is it?" Y'Juen said, jumping up himself.

"The Americans were the only ones who treated us right," Y'Tin responded.

"Then where are the Americans now?" Tomas asked.

The Americans were in America, as they all knew. Since they all knew it, why ask the question? The Americans had broken their promise to help them. Y'Tin knew it. He didn't know it for a long time. But now he knew it. Tomas and Y'Juen knew it, everyone in the village knew it. So why belabor the point?

Y'Tin decided that he would call Tomas and

Y'Juen "we" now in his mind, as one entity, as in "we doesn't know where the Americans are." Let them be "we." He would embrace their we-ness. He knew his father had done the right thing. His father had spent a long time thinking about it before joining the Americans. His father always spent a lot of time separating right from wrong. His ability to separate right from wrong was one of his main characteristics. He spent half his life thinking about it, just as his mother spent half her life thinking about the spirits. If "we" didn't know that, that was their problem. Its problem.

"Let's face it. Men like your father brought harm to the village," Y'Juen said. "My father never worked with anyone but his family."

"My father spends half his life separating right from wrong," Y'Tin said angrily. "He would never harm the village."

"Obviously, he's harmed all of us, including you. I have no respect for your father."

Y'Tin charged into Y'Juen's chest, bowling them both over. Y'Juen rolled on top of Y'Tin, pinning him down, but Y'Tin worked an arm free and threw a punch. Y'Juen ducked and Y'Tin's fist arced past him, hitting the hard ground. Pain shot through

142

his fingers. They wrestled for what seemed like an eternity before Y'Tin put a headlock on Y'Juen. He squeezed hard. He wanted to squeeze Y'Juen's head off, but the headlock didn't seem to be having much effect. Then Tomas grabbed Y'Tin by the back of his loincloth and pulled him off. He held Y'Tin's arms back, and Y'Juen used the opportunity to throw a lazy punch at Y'Tin's stomach.

"You're both too scared to fight by yourselves!" Y'Tin cried out. "The only way you two girls can win is if you gang up on me."

Y'Juen's face grew angrier, and he landed a second punch into Y'Tin's stomach. Y'Tin gasped for air.

"All right, all right," Tomas said. He let go of Y'Tin's arms and shoved him away. "Let's stop fighting." Y'Tin and Y'Juen locked eyes for a moment, and then Y'Juen walked away a few steps to cool off. Y'Tin closed his eyes to cool off himself. *We have to work together,* he said to himself. *We have to work together.* Tomas laid a hand on Y'Tin's shoulder, and Y'Tin tensed up. "Come on, we're all friends here. We can't be fighting."

Y'Tin couldn't sleep that night. His face grew hot as he thought of Y'Juen, so he tried to push his "best friend" out of his mind. Y'Tin decided that he couldn't forgive Y'Juen the way he usually did because Y'Juen had insulted his father. That was unforgivable.

Usually, the elephants formed a protective circle around Y'Tin, Tomas, and Y'Juen, as if the boys were calves in the wild. But that night Lady noticed Y'Tin awake and wandered over before falling asleep again. When Y'Tin sensed that Tomas and Y'Juen had also fallen asleep, a great relief washed over him. He wished they hadn't involved his father. Now he didn't feel he could ever be friends with them again, especially Y'Juen.

He tried to imagine what his father would do in the same situation. Once, his father had gotten mad at his friend Jake, but he never told anybody why. After that Ama was cordial to Jake, but Y'Tin could tell he never forgave him. He acted like he forgave him, but he really didn't. But another time Ama had gotten mad at his friend Y'Bier because Y'Bier had criticized Y'Tin's powerful auntie, who was Ama's sister. When Y'Bier apologized, Ama forgave him. So Y'Tin decided he might forgive Y'Juen if he apologized. On the other hand, maybe he would just pretend to forgive him. He'd have to wait until Y'Juen apologized before he decided. He thought about all this for a long time, just as his father would have. He thought and thought.

Lady suddenly issued a huge snorting sound. She used to sleep silently. But as her pregnancy progressed, she had started to snort. Jujubee also snorted when she slept. So no matter where Y'Tin slept, he would hear snorting. That was fate. He smiled to himself as Lady gave another big snort. Then he laughed out loud suddenly, thinking of the time that he'd first built the hutch. He had left some sugarcane inside, and when he got back from school that day, the hutch had been demolished and the sugarcane was gone. The other elephants had been working, which meant that Lady was the culprit. So he had to rebuild the hutch. He laughed almost like a lunatic, so relieved was he to think of a happy moment. All his thoughts about Lady were happy. He had never gotten mad at her.

Next Y'Tin thought of his mother and father—how hard they worked, how fiercely they loved him, Jujubee, and H'Juaih. He hoped his father was already fighting a guerilla war from the jungle. He believed it to be true. His father had once told him that belief came from the heart, intuition came from your gut, and reasoning came from your head. A "belief" meant what your heart thought was true, even if you had no proof. He believed in his heart that his mother and sisters were alive and that his father was fighting and, hopefully, winning. He figured if every man could kill three enemy soldiers, maybe the Dega would take back control of the Central Highlands. That wasn't too much to ask for, was it?

Y'Tin found the need to sleep overwhelming. Trying to stay up to think more just made him sleepier. A gunshot sounded from far away—Y'Tin had barely heard it. That was the last thing he heard before he fell asleep.

He dreamed of Jujubee. She was crying alone in the jungle, lost. Then there was a room, the ceiling slanted like in a longhouse, except it wasn't a longhouse. Then Y'Tin was in the room, counting bullets. He opened his eyes. It was dawn.

"You were talking in your sleep. Counting," Tomas said.

"I dreamed my sister Jujubee was crying."

Tomas rubbed his forehead for a moment. Then, "I'm worried about my family too. But my job now is to keep us and the elephants alive. I have a lot to think about, so you need to follow orders and not fight with Y'Juen. I thought you two were friends."

"We are. We were."

"Well, whether you're friends or not, you both need to follow orders."

Y'Tin paused before reluctantly saying, "All right." For now he would pretend to forgive Y'Juen. Later he would decide for sure what he would do. Y'Tin continued, "I was thinking. If we each kill three enemy soldiers, and every other Dega kills three enemy soldiers apiece, maybe we can win this war."

"We're not going to kill three enemy soldiers, Y'Tin. We don't even have guns."

"I'm a good shot with my crossbow. Maybe I can kill five, and you and Y'Juen can kill only two apiece."

Y'Tin had thought about killing a man before. After all, he had nearly killed a man when he went on that mission with Shepard. Everybody had thought about killing. This was, after all, a war. He was not afraid to kill a man. He was afraid only of a man killing him. His father had taught him that if you wanted to live in times of war, you should not fear killing a man, a woman, or even a child.

That day the boys started a systematic search for

the rest of their village folk. The search was in the shape of a fan instead of a circle. Y'Tin knew that if Tomas were a good tracker, he would want to make a circular search. He thought about mentioning this to Tomas but couldn't decide what to do. Actually, he had gone hunting with Tomas a few times and thought he was a pretty incompetent tracker. It had never mattered before, but now it did. Finally, about halfway through the day, Y'Tin announced, "We should really be making a circular search."

Tomas acted like he hadn't heard Y'Tin, although he was looking right at him. Tomas was clearly annoyed. Y'Juen said, "You're not in charge. Tomas is."

They were both incompetent trackers as far as Y'Tin was concerned. If they could read his mind, they would not like what they found. Y'Tin hated holding his tongue. He did not like worrying about everything he said to them.

They found many human tracks, but no fresh ones—the edges of the footprints were usually caved in rather than crisp and new. Also, there were only ten, twenty tracks in every trail they came across. So they couldn't have found their fellow villagers.

Every day they searched for fresher tracks, and every day they failed. Every day in their trek was different. Once, Y'Tin had seen some Special Forces soldiers playing chess. He hadn't understood why, with the same pieces in the same positions and with the same players, each game was so different. But now he understood. As they struggled to live in the jungle, every day was the same yet very different.

Then one day they found a huge number of footprints! At a glance it looked like two or three hundred people may have been making prints. Y'Tin's heart beat harder at the sight. He fell to the ground to examine the prints: They looked like they'd been made within the last week. "About a week old!" he exclaimed.

Y'Juen and Tomas slapped each other's shoulders. "It was a good thing we didn't listen to you!" Tomas said to Y'Tin. "It would have taken a lot longer to find this trail."

That deflated Y'Tin's elation a little, but he ignored Tomas. When they reunited with their villagers, he wouldn't ever have to talk to Y'Juen and Tomas again if he didn't want to. Frankly, he couldn't wait. And while it was true that they had found the trail in less than a week's time, Y'Tin knew that they were lucky to have found it without making a circular search. But there would be no convincing Tomas and Y'Juen of that now, so once again he held his tongue. What good was the truth when everybody thought you were wrong? He would have to ask his father about this someday.

That night he fell asleep and woke up abruptly in the black night. His heart was racing. He listened for a while but heard nothing threatening, so he drifted back to sleep. He woke up again to Tomas's calls. "Y'Tin. Y'Tin! Get up. Lady's missing."

Y'Tin sat up sleepily. How could an elephant be missing?

"Y'Tin!"

Y'Tin's head cleared, and he saw in the dawn light that Lady was indeed gone. He jumped to his feet and looked in every direction. "Where is she?"

"I woke up and she wasn't here," Tomas said.

At first Y'Tin wasn't sure what to do. How could you lose an elephant? But he saw her tracks clearly and started to follow them. She was making her own path through heavy jungle. What could have come over her?

He told the others he'd be back and jogged after her, easily following her path. An hour later he stepped into a clearing and there she was, grazing peacefully with the herd they'd seen before. She noticed him and hurried over. His relief at finding her instantly gave way to a flare of jealousy. His friends, his elephant—nothing was the same here in the jungle. Still, he would let her graze with them if it made her happy. But now that he was here, she didn't seem interested in the other elephants. He waited a moment to see what she would do, but she stayed by his side.

"Lady, *nao*," he told her. She docilely followed him, the way she always did. Once they rejoined the others, the boys found a creek and bathed their elephants. Then they began their search again. They were in high spirits, because it was just a matter of time now before they would find who'd made those tracks.

During a dinner of coconut and cooked bamboo, Y'Tin wondered whether his family was eating meat tonight. He wondered whether Jujubee was thinking of him. And he wondered whether they missed him. Y'Tin was used to missing Lady every day when he went to school. But for the first time

in his life, he missed his family. He had to believe
they were safe. But he couldn't shake free that
glimpse of a little girl crying by the fence. Even if
it wasn't Jujubee, he realized, it was another small
girl who could be dead now . . . who *was* dead
now.

That night as he lingered between sleep and
wakefulness, he could hear Tomas and Y'Juen
talking softly, but he couldn't make out what they
were saying. He opened his eyes and saw Y'Siu
sitting expressionless on one of the enormous
tree roots that stuck out of the ground. He sat
up. Y'Siu was looking at Dok. Then Y'Siu smiled
at her; he'd really loved that elephant. A rush of
affection for Y'Siu rose up in Y'Tin. Y'Siu was kind
of like a child, not a young man. He was uncom-
plicated, innocent. Next Y'Siu walked over to Dok
and laid his head on her trunk. But none of this
was possible because it was too dark to see Y'Siu
and Dok. Y'Tin lay back and closed his eyes and
still saw Y'Siu. Then Y'Siu disappeared, and Y'Tin
fell deeply asleep.

Chapter Ten

In the morning Lady was gone again. Y'Tin repeatedly hit the back of his head on the hard ground. He could not believe she was gone again. He looked immediately for her trail and began following it. After a couple of hours he heard trumpeting, and there she was—by a small lake this time—happy as she had been yesterday. Usually, elephant herds were made up of related female elephants. But for some reason this herd had accepted Lady.

And just like yesterday, when she spotted Y'Tin, she hurried over. Y'Tin almost wished he had his hook with him, so he could communicate how displeased he was. By the time he and

Lady got back to camp, they would all have lost several hours. But what did several hours matter anyway? If Tomas and Y'Juen were in such a hurry, they could just leave. He was a better tracker than either of them—just let them try to leave him and see what happened next. If they were tracking the wrong people, they might not be able to find the correct trail without Y'Tin.

He rode Lady back. When they reached camp, Y'Juen and Tomas both avoided his eyes. Tomas made a show of searching through his bag with his lips pressed together, and Y'Juen was preoccupied with stabbing a stick into the ground over and over. Their silence told Y'Tin how angry they were.

With only half a day of light left, the boys resumed their search. Tomas and Y'Juen still didn't speak to Y'Tin, and he followed behind them with Lady. It was a long, long day, and Y'Tin was exhausted. But the good thing was that they were putting distance between themselves and the wild herd. And at the same time they were getting closer to whoever had made the trail. Y'Tin felt satisfied that the wild elephants were far behind.

But after a restless night Y'Tin woke up to Tomas calling, "Lady! Lady!"

Y'Tin could see Lady a few meters away looking at him from where she stood in the dim dawn light. The jungle was even livelier than usual: Some animal, probably a wild pig, snorted just within hearing; several miniature rabbits scampered across Y'Tin's line of sight; a wild grouse clucked along the ground; and two ticks were trying to embed themselves into Y'Tin's right forearm. He picked up the ticks and squashed them between his fingers.

Y'Juen and Tomas simultaneously hopped to their feet and pounced on the grouse. Y'Juen came up with it. Meat! All thoughts of the trail vanished from Y'Tin's head. All he could think about now was meat. Then a second thought flashed through his head: Maybe Y'Juen would not want to share the meat with him. He wondered whether such paranoid thoughts were part of the changes a man went through in the jungle.

Lady wandered over. He climbed aboard her and simply lay on her back. When he'd first taken over handling Lady, he'd often have her *muk* so he could simply lie on her back. He had even gone hunting with her, lying atop her with his crossbow ready. He always felt safe up there. Even if he'd seen a tiger, he wouldn't have been scared. No animals' teeth could penetrate that thick hide. Humans were the only predator of elephants.

He wondered why Lady was so interested in the wild elephants. Maybe it had to do with her pregnancy. Maybe she knew that nobody in the village had ever been able to keep a baby elephant alive. Maybe she was only trying to do what was best for her calf. This was all guesswork for Y'Tin. All he knew was that he was jealous.

Tomas started a fire with the lighter Y'Juen had found before they escaped. As Y'Juen cooked the grouse on a spit he'd made, Y'Tin's mouth watered at the beautiful, wondrous smell of meat. While Y'Juen and Tomas ate, Y'Tin waited for someone to invite him to join them. They had almost finished before Tomas said, "Here, Y'Tin, you'll need meat to stay strong." Y'Tin slid off Lady and tore at the meat Tomas offered, chewing the ends off the bones before sucking out the marrow. For a moment he felt sorry for elephants, because they would never know the joys of eating meat.

Y'Tin turned sharply as something rustled the leaves, followed by the crack of a branch. He hopped to his feet. Two big elephants stood among the trees. They were easily recognizable as belonging to the herd Lady was so interested in. One had a very small tusk on her right side only, and another had no tusks and unusually large tan sections on her hide. Y'Tin caught his breath as Lady approached the elephant with one tusk. They touched trunks and sniffed at each other. Then the wild cow pulled off some bamboo leaves and started feeding. Lady pulled down an entire bamboo. Geng and Dok grew agitated, Dok rocking from her left to her right legs over and over as Y'Juen and Tomas tried to soothe her.

Y'Tin stared at the grazing elephants. He knew that if he called Lady, she would come. But she seemed so at home.

Tomas murmured to Geng and Dok in turn. Then he turned to Y'Tin, shaking his head. "You need to get Lady under control." Then he snapped, "Call her back. We need to get rid of these elephants before there's a fight."

"Lady!" called Y'Tin, and she ambled over.

After that Lady walked alongside Y'Tin, and though she didn't look back, Y'Tin was sure she knew that the two elephants were shadowing them, just out of sight.

Y'Tin was becoming depressed. He felt his depression in his aching stomach. According to his father, an ache in your gut was an instinct. But he didn't know what his instincts were telling him. He knew the two elephants had come for Lady. He didn't know how to get rid of them. Their tenacity made him depressed. A tiny yellow *cimbhi* chirped alone in a tree. He felt a sudden urge to squash that cheerful bird.

But Y'Tin didn't see or hear the wild elephants again, and several hours later he finally thought it was possible that Lady's new friends had abandoned her. Still, elephants could communicate over long distances, so for all he knew, Lady was still in contact with the herd.

When they broke early for camp, Tomas told Y'Tin, "We're going to go hunting for a while. Why don't you watch the elephants?"

Y'Tin had no idea when Tomas and Y'Juen had decided to go hunting. They seemed to have developed a knack for knowing what the other was thinking. Back in the village they'd hardly known each other. Anyway, Y'Tin didn't care what they thought of him . . . except he did care.

Friendship had always come easily to Y'Tin.

In fact, a year ago some of the boys in the village had decided to start a group. They called it Boys for Independence. It was based on the men's FULRO organization. When it came time for the boys to elect a chief, Y'Tin won every vote including his own.

After Tomas and Y'Juen left, Y'Tin felt relieved. He found a coconut and threw it to the elephants one at a time. They kicked it back—it was one of their favorite pastimes. After a while Dok kicked the coconut and it flew directly at Y'Tin. He fell to the ground to avoid it, but it clipped his forehead. He clasped his head. "Ah, Dok," he said. "Ahhhh." For a second there, he thought his skull was cracked. Lady came over to check on him. Then she walked away, so he figured he must be fine. Once, he broke his arm, and she had nudged at him lovingly over and over. Another time, he fell out of a tree, unhurt, and she barely noticed. So he felt she knew whether he was hurt badly or not.

When Tomas and Y'Juen returned to camp, they hadn't caught a thing.

And even though Y'Tin didn't say a word, Y'Juen snapped at him, "You had the easy job, taking care of the elephants." Y'Tin didn't answer, though the obvious answer was, *You're the ones who decided that I should stay alone with the elephants.*

Later, as darkness fell and they lay down to sleep, Y'Tin felt kind of sorry for Y'Juen, because now that they weren't friends anymore, Y'Tin didn't share the poncho with him. He must have been cold at night. Y'Tin wondered what they would do when the rainy season came in a couple of months. Hopefully, they would have found the others by then.

Tomas interrupted his thoughts. "We were thinking we need to move a little faster," he said. "You need to control your elephant. Next time you're gone that long, we won't wait for you."

Y'Tin felt very, very weary. When were Tomas and Y'Juen going to stop quibbling with him? "I'll try to get her under control if I have time," he answered. That sounded ridiculous even to Y'Tin.

"If you have time? What are you doing that's keeping you so busy?" asked Tomas.

"If I have time," Y'Tin said stubbornly. In the darkness he could feel Tomas and Y'Juen staring at him. He felt like an idiot, but what could he do? "We" was angry at him, and he hadn't even done anything.

Lady fell asleep standing, as usual. Y'Tin couldn't sleep, and in a couple of hours he heard movement and knew it was Lady, going to meet her wild friends. "Lady," he said, and the movement stopped. But he knew that as soon as he fell asleep, she would leave. He ached inside. The pain was all over him, not like the pain in his gut he got sometimes. It was strange. He felt almost as if he were levitating, as if the pain were a circle of air pressing against him. Heart, gut, head. Belief, intuition, reasoning. But what did it mean when pain pressed against you from all directions?

His heart filled with bitterness. He was bitter toward the North Vietnamese, the South Vietnamese, the French, and the Americans. Why must their battles include him? At that moment he hated them all, even the Americans his father had worked with and trusted, even the American nurse—whom Y'Tin had never met—who had chosen Lady's name before Y'Tin was born. The Americans had never helped the way the Special Forces had promised. And finally, he hated Yang Lie and Ai Die for cursing him by giving him a heart.

He woke to find Y'Juen and Tomas squatting

beside him, staring. "You were shouting in your sleep," Tomas said. Then he added, "Lady's gone again. She likes her new friends."

"I'm going to let her stay with them," Y'Tin said, and his words surprised even him. He hadn't decided until the moment he'd said it.

"What!" Tomas cried.

Y'Tin knew he was making the right decision, even though he hadn't thought about it at all. Still, he worried because he'd made the decision so quickly, unlike how his father made decisions. "It's the best chance for her calf to live," he explained to Tomas. "I'll stay with her for a week, until she gets more used to the herd. That way, I can be sure she can forget me."

"Elephants remember everything!" Y'Juen exclaimed. "You told me that."

"Are you sure?" Tomas asked. "We'll have to leave you. We can't stay here for a week."

"I understand," Y'Tin answered, meeting Tomas's eyes. "Go on. It's my fate."

Tomas and Y'Juen gathered their things. Y'Tin affectionately slapped Dok's hide. "No hard feelings for almost killing me with that coconut," he told her. She looked at him, and he was sure she was laughing. "Behave yourself, Dok." He and Tomas nodded solemnly for a good-bye. Y'Juen seemed confused, and something in his worried eyes reminded Y'Tin of how Y'Juen had been when they were still friends in the village. Then his eyes grew cold again, and he nodded to Y'Tin in farewell.

Y'Tin watched until they disappeared into the foliage. He fought against the urge to call out to them. He did not welcome being alone in the jungle. But if it was your fate, it was your fate. He felt some fear of being alone, but he also felt that relief again.

For the next few days, Y'Tin set up snares for small game and used his crossbow to hunt bigger game. That is, he planned to use his crossbow for bigger game. But he never spotted anything to shoot at. He did catch a rabbit on the second day, but then he remembered he didn't have a lighter. He'd tried to start a fire from scratch a number of times in the past but had succeeded only once. Now he spent an entire afternoon just preparing the tools: tinder, bow, nest, fireboard, drill. It was hard to find dry enough material. He drilled the fireboard off and on for several hours, then wondered whether it was safe to eat a raw rabbit. He was tempted. Instead, he sullenly ate coconut.

Three days went by, and Lady didn't return. Y'Tin knew it was time to leave. But he couldn't bring himself to do so.

He stayed another night, lying under the poncho. He thought over details from his life with Lady. He had begged his parents to let him work with elephants the first time he had petted Lady, but it took his father two years to say yes. Lady used to knock him to the ground with her trunk when she first met him. Then there was the time when Mountain was born. Even though Lady still knocked Y'Tin to the ground, and even though she still didn't listen to him, and even though she still wouldn't let Y'Tin brush her, she wouldn't let anyone but Y'Tin come near Mountain. Tomas had needed to chain their elephants elsewhere because of how touchy Lady was about her new calf. Mountain had liked watermelon, so every day Y'Tin had fed him one watermelon from the patch owned by Y'Siu's parents. When Mountain died, Lady lay on her side day after day, refusing to eat. Her ribs started to stick out, and Y'Tin was certain she was going to starve to death.

Then Y'Tin's mind returned to the present, and he wondered whether Y'Siu's parents sensed he was dead. He hoped he wasn't the one who would have to tell them. Y'Siu was their youngest child, and they doted on him. For instance, when Y'Siu had told them he wanted to be an elephant handler, they had said yes right then and there. They didn't even have to think about it.

Y'Tin couldn't comprehend how everything was so different from what it had been only a few weeks earlier. He ached for his previous life. He didn't understand how time worked. For instance, did the past matter or not? The future definitely mattered, and of course the present mattered. But the past was gone, never to return. So did it matter? He thought and thought about this, but he couldn't figure it out.

Y'Tin finally left. He packed up his gear and headed northwest, in the direction Y'Juen and Tomas had gone. He knew Lady would miss him. She loved him. He'd heard of other people who had found an elephant after many years of separation. So he might find Lady again one day. Or maybe she would find him.

He could not possibly have felt worse. That was the truth. He did not have a family, he did not have a friend, and he did not have an elephant. On top of that, the rain poured on him.

That night he fell asleep to the sound of the rain dripping on his poncho. When he woke the next morning, his poncho had fallen off his legs and his shins were so itchy that they felt inflamed. He sat up and examined them. They were so covered with mosquito bites that they appeared diseased. He had never seen anything quite like it. The itchiness was already driving him crazy. It was just one more thing making him miserable. He thought of something Shepard used to say: When it rains, it pours. That meant that if you put ground salt into a container, it would come out really fast. Every grain of salt stood for a detail in your life. And if they all came out really fast, that meant you had a lot going on in your life . . . or something like that. Actually, who cared what it meant? The Americans had never come to help as Shepard had promised.

The only good thing about the morning was that he didn't feel worse than he had the day before. He certainly didn't feel better, though. Still, he kept going.

The canopy was so heavy, the sun didn't show through clearly, so it was hard to tell directions. An American Special Forces soldier had brought a compass to the village once. It was truly magical the way it always knew the direction. The Americans could measure the invisible. And they liked to know all the facts, like exactly what time it was, exactly what temperature it was, and exactly what direction it was.

As he followed the trail, there seemed to be an awful lot of footprints—maybe five or six hundred—laid one upon the other in an ornate puzzle. He didn't bother to count as it would have taken him far too long. He thought the trail might belong to another village. But his intuition told him it was his fellow villagers.

He followed the trail day after day. When he closed his eyes, he saw footprints in his mind's eye. On the seventh day of following the trail, he saw many smaller trails coming and going, and he knew he must be close to camp. The tracks were fresh now, the edges of the prints crisp and clear.

Chapter Eleven

And then, abruptly, he was there. He was so excited that he started running at full speed, shouting out, "Ama! Ama!" though he didn't see his father. Then he stopped. He realized there were too many people—it couldn't be his village. But then he saw several members of the Buonya clan.

"Y'Tin! Y'Tin!" Y'Tin saw his father running toward him, and he broke into a run again. When they reached each other, they had both been running so fast that they collided. Ama embraced Y'Tin, who felt something like ecstasy to see his father. He held on to his father with all his strength. Then Ama picked him up, flipped him over his shoulder, and whirled him around. When his father finally let him down, Y'Tin could barely stand up because of his dizziness. The dizziness didn't bother him. It just seemed like part of his ecstasy.

"Y'Tin! My boy! We heard from Tomas and Y'Juen that you were alive. I went searching but couldn't find you." He lowered his voice. "Nobody is supposed to go searching for lost relatives. The commander shouted at me. He said if we all went searching, there'd be nobody here to fight."

"I was a week's walk away."

"Ah, that's what happened, eh? I was only able to search for a few days before the commander sent a man out to retrieve me. There were many tracks out there. The jungle has become crowded with fugitives."

Y'Tin looked around. "But where is Jujubee? Where are Ami and H'Juaih?"

"In the other camp. All the women with children are there. The women without children are here fighting alongside the men."

"But, Ama, when the North Vietnamese came, I thought I saw Jujubee at the gate all by herself."

"She was with me the whole time."

"Are you sure? Have you seen her?"

"Of course I have. She's safe with your mother."

Y'Tin let that sink in for a moment. That meant he had been haunted by a glimpse of the wrong little girl. That meant someone else's sister, someone else's daughter, was dead. He tried to think who it might have been, but his father began talking.

"Let's leave for the other camp now," his father said. "Your mother will never forgive me if we delay even a minute."

But Y'Tin wasn't quite ready to go yet. There were things he had to understand first. He looked around again. He didn't recognize many people. He spotted the Hlongs, of the heavenly cantaloupes, and the Nies, who enjoyed eating elephants. The camp was a mess—bags and weapons, blankets and baskets, all spread out beneath the towering canopy. They were on a plateau, hidden in the heavy bush, as if they were living in a large room in the middle of the jungle. A handful of old, torn tents had been erected, and a tattered flag hung on one of them. The flag looked exactly like a blanket that had been cut into a smaller piece.

"But, Ama . . . Ama . . ." Y'Tin wasn't sure what he wanted to say. It was just that he had expected everything to be okay the moment he found his fellow villagers. But now, looking around at the ramshackle camp, he knew that everything would not be okay after all. "Ama, what is happening? Did you make a sacrifice? Are the spirits unhappy? Are they punishing us?"

"Someday I'll understand all this," Ama said with determination. "But now—I don't know."

"Ama?"

"Let's walk as we talk, Y'Tin."

Y'Tin agreed, though he still had many questions. He pushed the bush away from his face and walked behind his father—they couldn't walk side by side because the foliage was too heavy.

In a few minutes Ama stopped, turned around, and spoke softly. "I wanted to leave before the commander noticed me. I'm going out on an action tonight, and the commander likes to practice first, the way the Special Forces did. First you practice, and then you go on a mission. But we need to go see your mother. She's been very upset about you being missing. Y'Juen's mother has been upset about you as well. She understands that to you, Y'Juen is your brother." Ama placed a hand on Y'Tin's shoulder and pulled him gently but firmly. "But why am I pausing? Let's hurry."

"Ama, wait!" His father waited, the furrows on his face looking even deeper than before. Y'Tin didn't know if it was an illusion caused by the lighting or if his father had recently aged. "Y'Juen and I are no longer friends," he blurted out. "We quarreled."

"About what?"

"Everything."

Y'Tin's father nodded as if he understood. "The jungle changes a man."

"Yes, I remember you said that." Ama thought and thought about everything, and then once he had decided something was true, he accepted it as a certainty. *The jungle changes a man.* "Ama? What will we do? All of us? What will become of us?"

"We'll fight the North Vietnamese and the Vietcong until we can't fight anymore. We have guns and go out on missions nearly every night. There are some good soldiers here."

"But how will we win?"

"We won't. Oh, we won't."

There was a long silence. Y'Tin knew that when his father next spoke, he would change the subject. He did that a lot. He would fall silent like someone submerging himself in water, and then he would resurface elsewhere.

Finally, Ama said, "I need to get you to your mother. We can talk on the way."

Y'Tin hesitated. It was all too much for his brain. He'd always wanted to be like his father, but suddenly, he felt like he didn't want to think and think, trying to figure out right from wrong and what would be or wouldn't be. That was for other men. He was an elephant handler.

Blood was already spilling out of the cuts and scratches Y'Tin was getting from pushing the bush away. He wiped blood off his face. "But what will become of Ami, of H'Juaih and Jujubee? If we lose the war, what will become of them?"

"I can't see the future, Y'Tin, unfortunately."

"Ama, what do you *think* will happen to us?"

"Perhaps the Americans will finally come to help."

"Do you think they will?"

"No. No, I don't. But it's something to hope for."

From the soldiers' camp, Y'Tin heard the sound of a *ding nam*. Shepard had always called it a flute. The Americans liked to make up their own names for things. Now Y'Tin turned to see who was playing, but through the heavy bush, he couldn't make it out. It was a melody Y'Tin had heard many times before.

It had always seemed like a happy song, but here in the jungle, the song now sounded sad.

"Y'Tin. Hurry. I'll need to get back for my mission tonight. And you'll get only one night with your mother and sisters. After that you'll need to return to the soldiers' camp. You'll be assigned a job by the commander."

Y'Tin felt a sudden outrage toward this commander. After all that Y'Tin had been through, he'd get only one night with Ami, H'Juaih, and Jujubee? "Who is this commander? And what kind of job?"

"He's from Ban Me Thuot. He worked with the Special Forces for many years. He's a good man. He's met Shepard," Ama said, as if meeting Shepard made the commander a good man. "You can be a messenger like Y'Juen, or a hunter or a cook."

"Where are Tomas and Y'Juen?"

"Tomas is in the other camp, with his mother. She's very sick with malaria and may die. Y'Juen is out on a job. Let's hurry."

"But, Ama, I don't understand. Isn't the purpose of war to win? Isn't that why people fight? Or is it because it's the right thing to do?" Ama didn't answer, just turned around and started walking. Y'Tin knew his father would stop in a moment with an answer.

After a while his father ran a hand through his thick hair and turned to Y'Tin. "To the Vietcong and the North Vietnamese, *they're* right. Who knows what's right?"

"But you always think about what's right or wrong!"

"It doesn't matter anymore," his father said fiercely. He grabbed both of Y'Tin's shoulders, shaking him once. "Sometimes, without even thinking about it, you step over a line, and on the other side of that line you find you've stepped into a situation you didn't want. Do you see? I didn't make a decision to fight; I made a decision to step over a line." Ama let go of Y'Tin but still leaned intensely forward. "Do you see what I'm saying?"

"I'm not sure."

"Maybe I stepped over the line years ago when I fell in love with your mother. How could I not fight for her now? Or maybe I stepped over the line just last month, when I knew the North Vietnamese were on the move and yet I didn't take my family away from the village."

"You mean you have no choice but to fight because you stepped over a line somewhere?"

"That's right. But son, son. Son. We need to hurry."

Once again Y'Tin followed as his father resumed walking. After a few minutes his father stopped again and turned around. He was frowning. His forehead reminded Y'Tin of one of those maps Shepard used to have, where the mountains looked like a piece of paper, folded and unfolded. "I need to tell you something. The commander is talking about eating Dok and Geng."

"What!" Y'Tin exclaimed.

"Y'Tin, the commander never worked with elephants. He doesn't feel the same way as we do. But he says he'll spare Dok and Geng if we can find the wild herd. Y'Juen told us about them. Do you think you could find them again?"

"But Lady's with them. She needs them. I don't know where they are . . . not exactly, anyway."

"I'm sorry about Lady."

Y'Tin suddenly wanted to cry about Lady leaving him. When he was with Lady, he had longed to be with family, and now that he was with family, he longed to be with Lady. He didn't see how he could be happy without both of them in his life.

"Y'Tin, there are thousands of Dega in the

jungle. Maybe tens of thousands. They're different from us, more Western. They think that the people from the remote villages are old-fashioned and less civilized. They think elephants are part of the old way."

"Old-fashioned? Us?"

"They wear Western clothes and smoke cigarettes that come in packages." Y'Tin didn't answer, and Ama changed the subject. "Y'Juen's mother is worried because he's late coming back. I was just thinking you might want to go find him. I'm very worried about him. Everyone is constantly worried now. It's very different from our life in the village. I thought I had worries before, but now I see those worries were nothing."

Y'Tin stared at the ground, concentrating. Y'Tin understood what his father said about worries. Previously, his only worry was keeping Lady happy. Now he was worried about every single thing. He could not think of even one thing that he wasn't worried about.

The jungle was dense and humid, filled with the smell of decaying vegetation. Y'Tin watched a slug the size of his hand make its way slowly away from his feet. Then he looked up at his father. He felt as tired as his father looked. They resumed walking, this time silently. Y'Tin's mind was a jumble of thoughts about all his new problems. There was the problem of the commander wanting to eat the elephants, the problem of his father thinking he could go find Y'Juen, and the problem of them losing the war. And, Y'Tin was sure, there were many, many other problems he couldn't think of at that moment.

When they reached camp, Y'Tin immediately spotted Ami, already running toward them. He cried out to her, and once again he broke into a run. He tried to embrace her, but she fell to his feet and threw her arms around his legs, weeping and saying, "I knew you'd come back to me."

He tried to lift her, but she clung to him. "Ami," he said. "Ami!"

His mother finally stood up and caressed his face, rubbing it almost as if she were trying to clean something off of his cheeks. Then she burst into tears again and wrapped her arms around his waist. "I didn't know you'd come back," she cried. "I don't know why I said that. I didn't know!"

Y'Tin held on to her the way he had when he was a young child. Before he and Y'Juen had escaped, he still thought of himself as a young child. Now he was a young man. He laid his head against her shoulder and felt comforted, but he felt something else, too—sadness that he was no longer a boy. He already missed his childhood.

Finally, Y'Tin's mother stopped sobbing. "Come and let me feed you," she said. She rubbed at his face again and even pulled at his skin as if trying to pull it off. It was actually a little painful. Before, when he was a boy, Y'Tin would have protested. But now he allowed her to pull at him.

"Don't pull off his face," Ama said gently, taking hold of her arm.

"Let me feed you both."

"I need to get back," Y'Tin's father said. "We're planning an action for tonight."

"But you just got back from an action yesterday!"

He leaned over and kissed her cheek, then turned to Y'Tin. "Spend some time with your mother. You can take a couple of days—I'll work it out with the commander. After that I'll be expecting you at the men's camp."

Y'Tin heard a birdlike screech and saw Jujubee running toward him. He knelt and she ran into him, bowling him over. He had expected that, but then for some reason she rammed a finger up his nose.

179

"Ow! Why did you do that?"

"Because I love you!" she cried out.

That made sense only if you were Jujubee. Y'Tin held her to him and rocked back and forth with his eyes closed. He felt at peace holding her that way. He heard a jangling sound approaching, and he looked up and saw H'Juaih. As always, she wore twelve rings on each of her ankles. She smiled shyly. She had become shy only last year. Many times when she talked, even to her friends and family, she would look down at her feet and smile a fleeting smile. He stood up and she hugged him primly.

His father slapped Y'Tin's shoulder. "I'll need to go now. I'll see you in a couple of days."

"Give him three days," Ami said firmly. When she spoke that firmly, no one ever crossed her. Y'Tin knew his father wouldn't argue.

"All right, three days," Ama said. He touched Ami's face before setting off. Even from the back, Y'Tin could tell how worried his father was. His shoulders slumped, and he walked with effort, like an old man.

As Ama walked off, Y'Tin looked around. Hundreds of people sat on the ground dwarfed by the giant trees. Here and there fruit hung from the

banana trees like decorations. Just a few meters away
Dok was pulling at some bark while Geng stood with
her eyes closed—Geng was very fond of sleeping.

There were as many people here as at the soldiers'
camp. Kids, old people, mothers, and sick people.
Directly opposite of where Y'Tin stood, he could see
about fifteen people lying on the ground. He knew
those were the sick people. Most of them probably
had malaria. Scattered everywhere were bursts of
color from the blankets. Blankets for the malaria
patients to lie over and under, for the babies to sleep
on, for the old people to wrap themselves in.

Ami said, "Come with me to our place. After I
feed you, Y'Juen's mother will want to talk to you.
You know how she acts like you're another son."
She lowered her voice. "But I know you don't love
her the way you love your family."

His family's "place" consisted of three bright
red blankets laid on the ground. Flies buzzed
around a covered pot—where had Ami gotten
a pot? She filled a bowl with what looked like
jungle potatoes in hot water and handed it to
Y'Tin. He was a little disappointed there was no
meat, but he didn't say anything. As he tried to
drink from the bowl, Jujubee clung to his left

arm. "Jujubee, let him eat!" Ami cried out.

Jujubee clung stubbornly to him. "Never mind," he said. "I'll use my right hand." He actually liked the way his sister clung to him.

Once his stomach was full, he suddenly felt exhausted. He knew his mother would want to talk, but he needed to lie down. Jujubee and H'Juaih lay on either side of him, each one clutching an arm.

When he woke up, it was already getting dark, and neither of his sisters was still lying with him. In fact, his sisters were nowhere to be seen. His mother sat watching him, and he had a feeling she had been sitting that way for a long time.

"Are you hungry again?" she immediately asked.

"No, no, I'm still tired. How long has it been?"

"A couple of hours. Some of the people from other villages carry clocks, so now we're always thinking about time."

Y'Tin's eyelids felt heavy and his head felt cloudy. "I need to rest," he said, closing his eyes again.

He woke up in the middle of the night under a blanket with Jujubee. Her snoring was even louder than he remembered. She couldn't do anything halfway, even snore.

He ached for Lady. He wondered how she was

doing. He hoped she was still with the wild herd. In the wild, female elephants always traveled in herds, while the males usually went off on their own. He had heard that some handlers worked with male elephants, but he had never seen that himself. It could have been just a legend.

He had always expected that he would work with Lady until she died. Then he would travel to Ban Me Thuot, to Thailand, to America. After he was finished traveling, he would open an elephant-training school in Vietnam. People would come from all over the country to work with him. But now he had no idea what he would do, where he would go.

There was a rare break in the leaves, and Y'Tin could see the sparkling *mtu*. His mind drifted to a song his mother had sung to him often when he was growing up:

> *The moon shines over, over you*
> *The sun shines over, over you*
> *The clouds shine over, over you*
> *My heart shines over, over you*

He remembered how safe and protected that song had made him feel, with his mother's heart shining over him. Even now, he would still feel comforted if she would come and sing to him. On the other hand, he was new to manhood, and he would not feel right asking his mother to sing for him. He had never seen a grown man make such a request of his mother.

He fell back asleep, and when he woke up, it was light out and his mother was sitting watching him again. She was holding a bowl, and as soon as he sat up, she said, "Eat more," and handed it to him.

He lifted the bowl to his mouth and drank the water, then used his fingers to eat the potatoes. This morning the soup also had some green plants he had never seen. His mother was a big believer in cooking green plants. She thought green food was the secret to long life, but all Y'Tin cared about was meat.

Y'Tin looked around. Tomas stood next to Geng, talking to her. Y'Tin felt a rush of anger. He doubted that he would ever forgive Tomas and Y'Juen for turning on him.

Then his anger turned to this "commander" person who wanted to eat the elephants. He could not understand that at all. Elephants were part of the civilized world, just like houses and schools and books. If this commander was so smart, he would know that. He would know that eating the elephants was the opposite of being civilized.

Y'Tin closed his eyes and concentrated on bringing back the past. After all, the shaman said that sometimes he could make things happen just by thinking about it. Y'Tin had never seen proof of this, but he did not think the shaman would lie. Y'Tin sat concentrating for a long time, but when he opened his eyes, his fate hadn't changed.

He saw that Tomas had left the elephants and was now leaning over someone covered head to toe in a blanket. That was his mother. Y'Tin wondered what Tomas thought about the commander's plan to eat Geng and Dok. Even if the soldiers ate two elephants, that would not feed them for long. Then they would be right back where they'd started. So what would they have achieved? Nothing—that was the truth. In short, he disliked the commander, and when he met him, he knew he would dislike him even more.

Y'Tin looked over at Y'Juen's mother. She was crying. *I hate Y'Juen,* he suddenly thought, and the thought surprised him. He had grown up with Y'Juen. But Y'Juen had turned on him.

High above, in the break in the leaves through

which he had seen the *mtu* last night, Y'Tin could see the blue sky. He stared at it and tried to soak in its beauty and let it soothe his bitterness.

He heard the sound of jangling and turned around to see his older sister.

"Y'Tin?" H'Juaih was looking at him.

"Yes?"

"Y'Juen's mother is sobbing," H'Juaih told him.

"Yes, I know."

"Y'Juen was supposed to go to the jungle north of here, carrying a message to another camp. He should have been back two days ago."

"Ama mentioned it," he said coolly.

H'Juaih looked confused, then her face fell. She was so compassionate that Y'Tin felt a rush of love for her.

"Y'Juen is good in the woods." He spoke "good in the woods" in English. It was the phrase Shepard used to describe someone who was an expert at negotiating the jungle.

"I know. That's what Ami told her, but she can't stop crying. Will you talk to her?" Now he knew why his father looked so tired sometimes and why he had so many lines on his face. It seemed that every day that passed carried more and more to agonize over.

Chapter Twelve

Y'Tin followed H'Juaih to the center of the camp. As they walked, Y'Tin began to dread that Y'Juen's mother would make the same suggestion that his father had—to go and search for Y'Juen. He was a natural candidate because he was such a good tracker and because everybody thought he and Y'Juen were best friends.

Y'Juen's mother was wrapped in a blanket. She was sobbing tearlessly, as if her eyes had run out of water. He hesitated, but then, as if she felt his eyes on her, she turned to him. "Y'Tin! Y'Tin!"

He squatted next to her, and she pulled him down and cried on him. They sat like that for a long time, until one of Y'Tin's legs fell asleep.

Holding her, feeling her ache for Y'Juen, he felt bad about how he and Y'Juen had fought. But the fact was, they had fought. He did not feel the way about Y'Juen as he had mere weeks ago.

Gut, heart, head. He searched for a feeling about whether Y'Juen was okay. But he couldn't find a feeling or a thought or an instinct to tell him. He didn't think it was time to panic yet, because in jungle time, a couple of days early or late didn't matter as much as it would have in a village. That's what his father had told him. When Ama had gone on missions with Shepard, he was never able to give the exact amount of time he would be gone. Sometimes he gave a time and it was wrong and other times it was right.

Y'Juen's mother did not say a word to him. She just held him and cried. Finally, he couldn't stand it anymore and exclaimed, "I'll go!"

She looked at him with confusion.

"I'll go search for him."

Her face filled with bliss, and when she started to cry again, he knew it was because she was happy and grateful.

"I'll go with you if you want," she said. "I'm not scared."

Y'Tin stared at the trees. Some of them were as tall as their houses had been long. "You don't have to come," he said. "I'll leave now, Auntie." He'd called her that for as long as he could remember. That meant he'd known Y'Juen for as long as he could remember.

She took his hand and rubbed it as she stared gratefully at him.

"If he's out there, I'll find him," he told her. In his head he thought, *Y'Juen is good in the woods, so he probably isn't lost.* If he'd been captured, Y'Tin wouldn't be able to help him. One second Y'Tin thought the most likely scenario was that Y'Juen had just gotten sidetracked, and the next second he thought he might have gotten hurt. Right this moment, he felt Y'Juen was merely sidetracked. But he had told Y'Juen's mother he would go in search of him, so he must. After all, it wasn't Auntie he had quarreled with, but Y'Juen.

Y'Tin trudged for an hour back to the soldiers' camp, where the men were busy eating. He saw his father sleeping and didn't wake him—he was probably exhausted from his mission the night before. But he spotted Y'Juen's father and went to him.

"Y'Tin!" he said warmly but tiredly, and Y'Tin wondered whether he had gone on the mission as well. Or maybe there were separate missions going on all the time.

"I told Auntie I would go search for Y'Juen."

"Y'Tin!" He pulled Y'Tin into a hug. "You're my second son. I wanted to go search for Y'Juen, but the commander wouldn't let me. All day soldiers are always asking him to let them go search for someone. He and I argued about it for an hour yesterday."

"Can you tell me where Y'Juen was going?"

"Several kilometers northwest of here. There's another camp there. I haven't been there, so I can't tell you more. Here, take my gun." He held out a rifle, but Y'Tin hesitated. It would just weigh him down, and he didn't know how to use it anyway. He remembered that mission he'd gone on, when he'd shot a bullet into the air. He had been lucky that he hadn't hurt anyone.

"No, I would probably just shoot my foot by accident," Y'Tin said, forcing a laugh. "I'll go now."

Y'Juen's father walked alongside Y'Tin until the camp was nearly out of sight. "Travel safely," Y'Juen's father said.

"Bye, Uncle."

Y'Tin took the path of least resistance, as Y'Juen probably would have. He concentrated on staying alert, to make sure to see, hear, or even feel any-thing unusual. The effort was exhausting.

It wasn't until midday that he spotted Y'Juen's tracks, not going north but south, returning to camp. That meant Y'Juen had already delivered his message and had somehow gotten waylaid on the way back. Y'Tin felt a moment of anger toward Y'Juen, and then he felt guilty for feeling that.

Y'Juen's footprints were easy to recognize because the sole of one of his shoes had a hole. But Y'Tin saw prints only when Y'Juen had stepped on bare ground, and most of the jungle floor was covered with vegetation.

Still, now that he knew the direction Y'Juen had been walking in, he was able to follow the trail even when there were few prints. When the tracks did show up, the footprints often lined up one next to the other, meaning that Y'Juen had paused over and over. If he hadn't paused, the tracks would be one after the other, not side by side. He searched for blood in the tracks but didn't see any. Instead of anger, he now felt worry. Y'Juen was either sick, injured, or exhausted. Or maybe all three.

Y'Tin drank from his canteen and continued his journey. It was late in the afternoon when he spotted a body in the distance and knew immediately that it was Y'Juen. Y'Tin cried out at the sight, ran closer, and touched the body: warm. His heart leaped as he felt the warmth. He would not wish any Rhade dead, whether it was a friend or not.

Y'Juen lay facedown. Y'Tin tapped his back. "Y'Juen? Y'Juen!" But Y'Juen didn't respond. Y'Tin flashed on how Y'Juen's mother had sobbed and sobbed. He felt a pulse on the wrist and wondered what to do next. If it were a hurt elephant, he would search first for the wound that must be there. He didn't see anything on Y'Juen's back, and he didn't think it was a good idea to turn over the body . . . the person . . . Y'Juen.

But if it were an elephant, he would turn over the body if only he could. Anyway, Y'Tin was going to have to move Y'Juen to get him back to camp; that is, unless he determined that it was better to go get help. But he didn't have the slightest idea how he would make such a determination.

There might be some blood that he needed to stanch the flow of. That settled it; he would turn over the body. He did so as gently as he could and saw the wound: a bruise on Y'Juen's forehead that formed a circle almost as wide as a fist. Y'Tin's hands began to shake at the sight of the wound. He looked around and noticed signs of a fight: injured plants . . . broken twigs . . . a second set of footprints. He felt his heart pounding. It felt like his chest was heaving inside and out. Now he knew why Y'Juen had been pausing so much: He was being tracked and needed to freeze when he heard his tracker. But the tracker had finally caught up with him. . . . Panic was rising in Y'Tin, and he didn't know what to do about it.

There was some daylight left. Not a lot, but enough to go a short way. No need to go get help— the only justification for that would be if there seemed to be broken bones, like, say, a broken back. But Y'Tin trusted that he would not aggravate a head wound by picking Y'Juen up. He grunted with the effort of hauling Y'Juen onto his shoulders. *Unh!* He weighed more than he looked like he would.

Y'Tin struggled with every step. When he'd gone on that mission with his father and Shepard, Shepard had carried Ama's friend without any apparent effort except for the sweat that had broken out on his forehead. If Shepard could carry a man, then Y'Tin could surely carry a boy. But Y'Juen was so heavy.

With each step, Y'Tin wondered whether he was capable of taking another. He had never thought it would come to this—Y'Juen's life depending on him. It was too much responsibility! He walked until the sun set. He considered walking farther, even in the darkness, in what he thought was the right direction. He was very tempted to try, but he knew that if he went in the wrong direction, that would mean he would get Y'Juen back to camp even later. And maybe not just later, but too late. So he stopped. He meant to lower Y'Juen gently to the ground, but he accidentally thumped him down. That made him feel thoroughly incompetent. Again he wondered whether it would be better to go for help, and again he rejected the idea. "I'm sorry I dropped you. I'm doing my best," he mumbled, and was surprised when Y'Juen answered.

"What?" Y'Juen said. "What?"

"Y'Juen, it's Y'Tin!" But Y'Juen didn't say more. Y'Tin wrapped his poncho around Y'Juen and then lay on the ground next to him, on top of those succulents that covered much of the jungle floor. His teeth chattered in the cool night. How had life come to this? How?

He remembered the way he and Y'Juen used to play together. Y'Tin could run and kick harder, but Y'Juen could kick more accurately. The earliest memory he could recall dated back to age four, but his mother had told him they'd been friends since they first started walking. Then Y'Tin thought about just a week and a half ago, when Y'Juen had insulted Ama. He hadn't thought he would ever forgive Y'Juen. But there, right there on the jungle floor, he forgave him. He could not blame Y'Juen for looking up to the older boys. That is, he *could* blame Y'Juen, but what would that get him?

And Y'Tin remembered again his father's adage: The jungle changes a man. Ama had been trying to explain to Y'Tin why people needed houses instead of just living in the bush. Y'Tin didn't see what difference it would make. After all, he slept every night in his hutch, which was more like a tent than a house. But Ama had explained that people acted different in the jungle—without houses, villagers became less civilized. "Even your hutch preserves your civility," his father had said. Y'Tin was always impressed when his father got philosophical that way. In short, Y'Juen, Tomas, and even Y'Tin had changed when they were in the jungle together.

"What?" Y'Juen said again. "What?"

Y'Tin didn't answer, just stared into the darkness, worrying about his best friend.

Chapter Thirteen

In the morning Y'Juen seemed to have gained weight. Y'Tin's neck and back ached like crazy, but he kept going anyway. He made slow progress, and it got slower the closer he got to camp. War was so much more tiring than daily life. He knew his father might find that thought naive of him, but Y'Tin had not realized just what war consisted of. War was exhausting. These last few weeks had depleted all of Y'Tin's reserves. He did not think he would be good for anything when he got back, least of all becoming a messenger. He felt irate at the thought of the commander giving him a job as soon as he got back. If the commander tried that, Y'Tin would have to tell him no. That was all there was to it.

When he finally reached the soldiers' camp, he set Y'Juen down, again harder than he meant to. Ama was already running toward him. He saw a number of men looking at the body, but they seemed hardened, uncaring.

Instead of saying hello when his father arrived, Y'Tin said, "He's alive. But his breathing is uneven. He—"

"Let me get his father," Ama interrupted. "Go tell his mother."

"But who will take care of him?"

"We have a doctor from another village. Now go."

Y'Tin ran off. Without Y'Juen on his shoulders, he felt free and light. It seemed like only half an hour before he reached the women's camp. He went straight to where H'Juaih was sitting with Y'Juen's mother, comforting her. Y'Juen's mother looked up at him with fear in her eyes.

"He's alive," Y'Tin said. He opened his mouth to say more but couldn't think of what else he wanted to say.

Her face was a mix of terror and joy as she jumped to her feet and set off toward the men's camp.

After that Y'Tin wanted to be a hunter for the village, not a messenger. He did not want anyone carrying him on their shoulders. Plus, if he was successful, he could provide meat for the men and help steer the commander away from the idea of eating the elephants. If only he knew how to use a gun.

He went to see his mother, who was now sitting with H'Juaih. Jujubee was laughing with one of the other young girls. Y'Tin tried to remember the last time he saw someone laughing, but he couldn't.

Ami hugged him and rubbed at his face again. She had never done that before the village take-over, but now she was doing it regularly. "One of the soldiers found some rice in an abandoned village. Have some."

She dipped a cup made from bamboo into a pot and came up with steaming rice. Y'Tin gobbled it down. He hadn't eaten rice since he was digging that hole in the cemetery. After that thought, the rice tasted less good, but he ate it just the same.

He ate several cups of rice and then lay down to nap. Sleeping after a meal of rice was probably as good as it got during a wartime.

"Are you going to tell him?" H'Juaih asked Ami.

Y'Tin didn't know what that meant, but he knew it wasn't good. And he knew the last thing he felt like hearing was something that wasn't good. But he looked at his mother and asked, "What?"

"The commander has decided to take the elephants tomorrow for the soldiers to eat."

Y'Tin suddenly didn't feel tired anymore. He told his mother that he was going hunting right that second. He picked up his crossbow. "I'll need to catch something big," he said. He thought that, if necessary, he would take down a wild elephant to save Dok and Geng. He didn't know if he could do that with a crossbow, but he would worry about that later.

"Y'Tin, the commander has already decided," H'Juaih said.

"Then I'll have to change his mind. I need to hurry. I have to get something big before tomorrow." Some thoughts flashed in his head. For one thing, he wondered why the people from his village weren't protesting this idea of eating the elephants—*their* elephants. For another thing, he wondered if he could hunt now. He hadn't gotten much sleep or rest in a couple of days, and he wasn't sure he could even

199

stay awake. But he had to save Dok and Geng.

H'Juaih stared disbelievingly at him. "You just got back!"

"I have to do this," he said. He thought of what his father had said about crossing a line. He had crossed a line years ago when he had decided he wanted to work with elephants someday. Because of crossing that line, he now had to *kill* an elephant. It didn't make sense, but there it was.

He spotted Ama running toward them and thought, *What now?* He stood up to greet him, not really wanting to hear what his father was going to say.

But when his father reached them, Ama laid a hand on Y'Tin's shoulder and said, "It's Y'Juen. He's all right. He woke up. He's talking. I just wanted to let you know."

"Ama," Y'Tin said, and laid his head on his father's shoulder.

He stayed like that for several minutes, until his father said gently, "I need to get back to the other camp. But Y'Juen's mother wanted me to thank you. She would do anything for you now."

"She doesn't have to do anything at all."

Ama caressed Ami's face, as he often did in parting, and then headed back, Jujubee walking with him to the edge of camp. Y'Tin watched, wanting to go hunting but also wanting to stay and rest.

"I may be gone overnight," Y'Tin told his mother. "Don't worry about me."

"Y'Tin. Y'Tin, you just got back."

"I don't want to do this, but I have to."

He set off and walked through the jungle for a couple of hours. He picked a spot near a river where animals might come to drink. The branches in the trees were so high up, there was nowhere for him to climb. Instead, he lay in the heavy bush. He knew he might have a long wait—he'd probably spooked any animals around with his human scent. On the bright side, he was situated between where an animal might approach and the river, and he was upwind. He waited with his crossbow. Hunting was a lot about waiting.

The more silent he was, the more still he was, the more alive he felt. He didn't let his mind wander, just aimed every part of his insides and outsides at that pathway. When it began raining, he thought about giving up. He was sick and tired of everything going against him. But he wasn't going to give up. This was too important.

The rain fell harder and harder through the foliage. Trying to stay optimistic, he thought about how the rain would mask his scent as well as any noise he might make. So he waited. Once, he had waited in a tree for five hours and gave up only because it was getting dark.

The only problem was that he was getting awfully itchy. It was all in his head—it happened to him quite a bit. It happened when he was hunting, and it happened in school. Monsieur Thorat would be talking on and on, looking directly at the class, and Y'Tin would grow itchier and itchier.

He moved just his toes, thinking maybe a little movement would somehow make the itchiness go away. Even his scalp felt itchy. Monsieur Thorat always told him to concentrate on *not* being itchy. So now he took a big breath and told himself, "You are not itchy. You are not itchy." But focusing his attention on the itchiness just made it worse. He was so itchy, he wanted to scream. He decided to focus on how good it would feel when he was finally able to scratch.

Y'Tin was so soaked, he worried that his fingers might slip off the bow, and he was so itchy, he wanted to scratch himself bloody. But he had a sense that an animal would be passing through soon. And, suddenly, there it was—a beautiful buck, at least several years old judging by its antlers. When the buck walked into range, he pulled back the arrow and shot. Missed! He set up again but couldn't get a second shot off before the buck had bounded away. How could he have missed that first shot? It was a perfect setup. So all the waiting was for nothing, and now he'd spooked the buck. He scratched his legs for a full minute, then scratched his whole body. Fate was not with him right now.

The rain eased up as he headed back to camp. Halfway there, he noticed buck marks on some tree bark. His father had taught him that bucks rubbed on a tree with their antlers and cleared leaves on the ground to mark their territory. He decided to try once more. He found a small tree he could climb into and sat with his crossbow and arrows. He waited and waited and began to wonder whether he was wasting his time. He knew it wasn't his fault; everybody went through periods when the *k'sok* and *m'tao* were chasing you and nothing you attempted would work out.

After a while Y'Tin could barely keep his eyes open—that happened a lot in school as well.

Whenever it happened, he was sure that Yang Lie was testing him, trying to make him fall asleep. But he would not give up. He willed himself to keep his eyes open and outlast the buck, just as he always outlasted Monsieur Thorat. He couldn't keep his eyes open, though, and he dreamed that he was sleeping in his hutch.

The next thing he knew, he was in motion. He thumped to the ground. At first he thought it was a dream, since he often dreamed of falling. But the pain was real. His whole body was sore at the same time. All of it. Every bone. Every muscle. He groaned. He cursed Yang Lie.

He realized that it didn't matter whether all of this was his fault or the spirits'. The fact was, one way or another, he had become totally useless. At that very moment he couldn't even get up. But that worked out great, because he didn't *want* to get up. He lay there for several hours as the jungle grew dark. He worried that a tiger might come, and he didn't even have the will to protect himself. On the other hand, why protect himself? He wished a tiger would come and end this all right here. Even his mother would forget him, just like Lady had. He was totally, totally useless.

Chapter Fourteen

Y'Tin fell asleep right where he was. He awoke with a start. A snake was slithering across his face. He pushed it away and sat up. But the snake was back. He pushed it away again. Then he didn't feel the snake anywhere around him.

But he heard something. A familiar snort. No. His ears were playing tricks on him. But he heard it again. That snort. He waited, and what he'd thought was a snake touched his face again. "Lady!" he cried. "Lady!" She ran the tip of her trunk across his face, and he started crying.

"Thank you for coming. Thank you." Then his crying turned into sobbing. He had never sobbed in his life. His sobs shook his body. It was as if he were possessed. Lady seemed to be trying to figure out what was wrong with him.

When his sobbing let up, he babbled to her, "I was all alone. I fell out of a tree. But it's not that bad." She rubbed her trunk along the top of his head, still trying to ascertain what was wrong. Then she went back to sniffing his face. "Did you come back because you knew I was miserable, or were you coming back anyway? Never mind. It doesn't matter." He reached up to clutch her trunk.

He heard something moving a few meters away and feared the worst. But Lady was calm, so maybe it was just a mouse or a lizard. *"Muk."* She knelt down and he climbed on her and lay there until morning, soaking in her Lady-ness. Maybe it was just his imagination, but his pain seemed to start ebbing as he lay there.

Daylight came slowly, and still he didn't move. He closed his eyes but didn't sleep. "Lady," he murmured. "You—" He stopped short and opened his eyes at a noise. "Lady . . ." A couple of meters away stood a baby elephant.

He forgot to have Lady kneel as he slid to the ground. He fell over but never took his eyes off the calf. Lady leaned over her baby, then ran her trunk on his face. Her face. A girl. "Your baby." He forgot about the pain in his body. "It's your baby."

He stared at the calf. The calf stared at him. She looked so small. He remembered how big Mountain had been. This new calf was so much smaller that worry washed over him. He was taller than she was. He tried to approach her, but she reared back on her hind legs in fear. He could smell her: a smell almost like dirt, like rich soil. Tufts of hair stuck up from the two humps on her head. Her eyes were the color of the tea Shepard used to drink by the liter. Y'Tin wanted to do something—anything—to help out, but he didn't know what to do. He considered mashing up a banana for the calf but rejected that idea. There was a reason baby elephants had no grown-up teeth. They were meant to nurse. But he had to do something. He spun around help-lessly, looking for something to do. "Let's go get some water," he said. "*Nao*, Lady!"

Lady walked obediently. When he looked back, he saw that her baby was following a few meters back. He waited for the calf to catch up, but when he stopped, she stopped. Then he started walking backward, and she started walking again. Then he stopped and she stopped. He did that once again, just for fun, and then he turned around and walked, confident that Lady and the baby were following him.

When they reached the river, Lady filled her trunk over and over. The calf walked under Lady and started filling her trunk from there. Y'Tin gulped at the water. He hadn't realized how thirsty he was. That was the positive side of being miserable; it made you forget your thirst. When the baby had finished drinking, she submerged her head a moment and then lifted it up. She sprayed water at Lady, then opened her mouth as if to trumpet. Instead, a squeaky noise came out of her.

Y'Tin waded into the river, turned over, and floated on his back. Lady playfully sprayed water on him while he laughed. It felt good to laugh. It was amazing the way Lady could make him feel miserable by going away and make him feel happy by coming back. It was not good to love something during a war. That was the truth. But it was also not good *not* to love anything during times of peace. Hmmm. So maybe if you thought there might be a war, you should try not to love anything . . . or in war you should try to . . . It was all too confusing for Y'Tin.

Anyway, he decided to name the baby Mtu because she was as beautiful as a star.

Y'Tin wanted to stay out here with the elephants, but he knew if he didn't return, his mother would be frantic. On the other hand, the elephants would be in danger if he returned to camp. But on the other hand of *that*, if he took Lady and Mtu to the mothers' camp, the commander wouldn't know. Then he could tell his mother he was safe and decide what to do next. So he rode Lady into camp. He sat up extra tall as everybody fussed over Mtu. The children all crowded around the baby, exclaiming how beautiful she was. Y'Tin slid off Lady to protect Mtu. She hid under her mother and took baby steps while Lady took big steps.

He didn't know many of the people in the camp. And he didn't know any of the guards. He realized that even if his villagers refused to eat the domesticated elephants, people from other villages would eat them in a second. Maybe it was Y'Tin's imagination, but one of the guards seemed to be looking hungrily at Lady and Mtu. In fact, all of a sudden, *everybody* seemed to be looking hungrily at the elephants. Dok and Geng were gone.

"Stand back!" he cried out to the children crowding Mtu. "You're scaring her." The kids took a step back, but then immediately started crowding the elephants again. He saw Jujubee tearing across camp. When she reached the elephants, she suddenly got all gentle and talked softly. Y'Tin was impressed with how gentle she became. He had never seen her like that before. Still, Mtu leaned her body away as Jujubee reached out.

Ami and H'Juaih came over and oohed and aahed over Mtu. Then the guard headed over. Y'Tin felt a moment of panic and considered making Lady run away. But he decided it was better to stay calm. No need to get everyone overexcited. When the guard approached, Y'Tin said, "She's scared of people."

"How much would you sell the calf for?" the guard asked.

Why would the guard want to buy a calf if not to eat it? Y'Tin could not think of another reason.

"She's not for sale," he replied.

Y'Tin told his mother he would be gone for a few days, explaining that he wanted to spend time with Lady and Mtu, just the three of them.

"And then what?" Ami asked.

"I don't know," he answered. "I need to . . . I need to think."

She stared so intently into his eyes that he felt as if she could see inside his brain. If she could, then she understood a lot more than he did. Then she said helplessly, "You're just like your father."

Y'Tin didn't understand. He was nothing like his father. But he didn't try to fathom what she was talking about. That was for another day.

He set off, taking his hook. They walked for several days. He kept trying to touch Mtu, but she wouldn't let him. He wondered why Lady couldn't communicate to her calf that it was safe to let him touch her. But, then, why did he really need to touch her? He didn't need it, he just wanted to touch her more than anything in the world. She was so happy that he almost felt as if touching her would make him happy as well.

He loved traveling with Lady and Mtu. It was only at night when he thought of Geng and Dok. Every night he wondered, *Are Geng and Dok still alive?* On the fourth night he suddenly felt deep inside himself that they were dead.

The next day Y'Tin decided to stop when they

came to a small waterfall. One of his favorite memories was when Y'Siu, Tomas, and he had taken the elephants to a lake, where Y'Tin saw elephants swim for the first time. They were surprisingly graceful in the water. He thought back to when he was still in training. Tomas had told him that many, many years ago, elephants knew how to fly. He hadn't believed Tomas, but when he saw the elephants swimming, it was exactly as if they were flying. So what did Y'Tin know?

Mtu, however, still had a lot to learn about water. She approached the waterfall suspiciously. She stuck her trunk into the waterfall and then quickly withdrew it and stepped backward.

Lady lay on her side while Y'Tin scratched her hide as hard as he could. Then he reached out to scratch Mtu, but she hopped away. He had never seen an elephant hop before!

Later, while Mtu was nursing, she let Y'Tin stroke her bristly neck. She had more bristles than her mother, and they were softer. Tomas believed that elephants would live longer if you stroked them sometimes as they ate. He had learned that from the man who had trained him, who had learned it from the man who had trained *him*. And so on, Y'Tin supposed. Someday when he trained other elephant handlers, Y'Tin would pass along this belief. Someday . . .

He knew he could not bring Lady and Mtu back to the camp again. Even if he could trust his own villagers not to eat the elephants, he would not be able to influence the commander. He had still never seen the commander, but he liked him less and less every day. So Lady and Mtu needed to bond with the wild herd. That was Mtu's best chance to live. Y'Tin thought about how he had always planned on mashing food for Lady when she got old, so she wouldn't starve when her last set of teeth wore down. He had promised her he would never let that happen to her, but now he realized that you could not always keep promises during times of war.

They spent six glorious days at the waterfall. Y'Tin had experienced many happy days in his life, but he thought these were the happiest. It was weird that the happiest days could come in the middle of a war. Go figure, as Shepard would say. At first he thought that happiness didn't solve many problems, but then he realized it could solve problems after all. It solved the problem of what exactly he should do next. He couldn't keep the elephants. He could not keep them alive. He simply didn't know how.

On the morning that he decided to send them away, they performed their usual routine: playing in the waterfall, brushing Lady's hide, petting Mtu. The morning passed quickly. He wondered whether he should spend a few more days with them. What was the hurry? But every day he grew more attached to them, and he knew that soon he would not be able to send them away. If he didn't send them away, he would have to stay with them in the jungle. Keeping Mtu alive would be his responsibility. But no one he knew had ever kept a baby elephant alive. Much as he would have liked to believe he would be the first, he just didn't know if it was true. Even Tomas's trainer, the legendary elephant handler James Bya, had failed several times to keep a calf alive. And James Bya was supposed to have been the best elephant handler the village had ever had. Some people thought he was the best elephant handler who'd ever lived, though Y'Tin didn't see how anyone could know such a thing. Like Y'Tin, Bya had not used a hook. Unlike Y'Tin, the elephants always loved him from the first moment they met him.

He had planned to send Lady and Mtu away right after he brushed Lady down, but as the day wore on, he couldn't bring himself to do it. He was growing weaker and weaker every moment. Finally, in mid-afternoon, he closed his eyes for several minutes, just staring at the darkness inside his eyelids and concentrating as hard as he could. He didn't know if he had the strength to do it. Then he opened his eyes.

"*Nao,* Lady! Lady, *nao!*" he suddenly shouted. Lady sniffed at his face. He stepped back and said, "No!" Then he called out "*Nao!*" again, this time using the hook. Lady turned uncertainly and took a couple of steps before pausing to look at him. If he cried, she would come back to check on him, so he fought back tears. "*Nao,* Lady!" He waved the hook, and Lady and Mtu walked slowly off. He ran as fast as he could in the other direction. He wanted to run into a tree and bang his head on it until his skull cracked.

When he lost his breath, he stopped and laid his forehead against a tree. Instead of banging his head, he tapped it over and over on the rough bark. He thought about the camp and knew he couldn't stay there, fighting a war that they would surely lose. He decided he would gather everything he might need for the journey to Thailand, where he might be able to find work involving elephants. His mother would be devastated. But his future did not lie in the land he loved. That was too bad. But that was war.

When he caught his breath, he headed to camp. The jungle was so thick, he couldn't see more than a few meters in front of himself. He smiled suddenly, as if he had been touched by Lady's trunk. He would never see her again. He suddenly just knew it, the way the shaman knew things. But Lady and Mtu would live. He knew that, too. That was the truth.

Author's Note

It's always a revelation to write a new book and learn about lives so different from my own. My research began with reading about hunting, tracking, elephants, Dega, and the Vietnam War. But I wanted a different kind of information than those books could offer. So I traveled to the San Diego Zoo to spend time with Asian elephants and their keeper (the elephants were intelligent, emotional, and capable of profound bonds with humans). I also traveled to North Carolina three times to interview Montagnard refugees living there, including a former elephant handler. I sought help from a retired Special Forces soldier and even scrubbed an elephant's hide at a place called Have Trunk Will Follow.

Still, novels by definition are fiction, and subject to the demands of storytelling. There were many facts that could not fit and I want to share some with you here. In Vietnam, the indigenous people of the Central Highlands call themselves "Dega" (or "Degar"). This is the term I use in the book, although in the United States, most Dega immigrants call themselves "Montagnard," which is French for "mountain people."

The Montagnard tribe I write about is the Rhade (Rah-day). To my knowledge there is no Rhade-to-English dictionary. As a result, different sources contradict one another about spelling and meaning and even about certain aspects of Rhade culture. For example, two sources said the Rhade houses were built facing north to south, but another source said the houses were built facing east to west. It's possible that different Rhade villages have different customs.

In the novel, the characters often comment on the promise the Americans made with the Dega: to return and help with the war if the North Vietnamese violated the Paris Peace Accords. Sadly, the promise was never fulfilled. Many Montagnards risked their lives by helping the American Special Forces, and in doing so made their villages more vulnerable to enemy attack once the Americans pulled out. Hard numbers are difficult to come by, but half of all adult male Montagnards are thought to have lost their lives fighting with the Special Forces during the Vietnam War. Many more died when they were left to fight on their own.

The US Special Forces did honor their relationship with the Dega in another way. More than 9,000 Montagnards have immigrated to the United States, mostly settling in North Carolina, the state where the Special Forces have their headquarters. Retired Special Forces soldiers purchased 110 acres of land in the area for the Montagnard Americans to turn into a cultural center and raise crops.

Different sources contradict one another, but there seems to be general agreement that since 1975, the overall population in Vietnam is burgeoning, while the Montagnard population is stagnant or decreasing. The Vietnam government claims that its policies toward the Montagnards are humane, but there have been reports of forced sterilizations and assimilation, religious persecution, torture, and even killings.

Meanwhile 9,000 men, women, and children are building their futures in the United States, like so many dispossessed people before them.

A Million Shades of Gray
by Cynthia Kadohata
Reading Group Guide

Discussion Questions

1. Discuss Y'Tin's attitude toward school. Why is his mother so determined that he complete his education? Cite evidence that Y'Tin is willing to learn in spite of his rebellion against school. When the North Vietnamese become a threat to the Rhade tribe, Y'Tin's family is forced to leave the village. Explain why Y'Tin suddenly wants to go to school when he no longer has to.

2. Y'Tin spends a lot of time daydreaming and thinking. He explains the difference to his mother: "Daydreaming is thinking about things that aren't true yet. Thinking is when you ponder matters that are already true." What "truth" does Y'Tin ponder the most? Which "truth" hurts the most? Debate whether Y'Tin's daydreams come true. Discuss Lady's role in helping Y'Tin realize his dream.

3. Y'Tin says that next to his father, Tomas is the man that he most admires. What is it about Tomas that Y'Tin admires? What causes Tomas to turn on Y'Tin? How does this change Y'Tin's admiration for Tomas? When do Tomas and Y'Juen become "we," casting Y'Tin aside? Y'Tin's father has always told him the jungle changes a man. Debate whether it's the jungle that changes Tomas and Y'Juen, or something else.

4. Y'Tin thinks a lot about betrayal. Debate whether the Rhade feel betrayed by the Americans. How do Tomas and Y'Juen have a different idea of betrayal from Y'Tin? Tomas and Y'Juen think Y'Tin's father betrayed his people. Debate whether Y'Tin's father was actually working on behalf of his people. Y'Tin says he would rather die than betray his people. Discuss whether Tomas and Y'Juen would make that pledge.

5. Explain what Y'Tin's father means when he says, "We must use the jungle as a weapon."

6. At the beginning of the novel, Y'Tin is a boy, and at the end he is a man. At what point does he realize he has become a man? Y'Tin feels sad he is no longer a boy. What does he miss most about childhood? What might Y'Tin say was the toughest part about becoming a man?

7. Early in the book, Y'Tin refers to Tomas as a man. Discuss whether Tomas displays the qualities of manhood. How is Y'Tin a bigger man than Tomas and Y'Juen?

8. Fear overtakes the Rhade tribe as the North Vietnamese and the Vietcong threaten their village. Y'Tin's father tells him that he has to face what's happening. When Y'Tin says he isn't scared, his father replies, "Then you're not thinking straight." Why is it important for Y'Tin to feel fear? How might fear keep Y'Tin focused and cautious? Discuss other times when Y'Tin comes face-to-face with fear. How does he deal with each situation?

9. Explain why Y'Tin's father calls the war the American War. Why are the North Vietnamese especially interested in men like Y'Tin's father? How does his father's work with the Americans make the entire Rhade tribe vulnerable?

10. Y'Tin's father worries that the North Vietnamese might capture Y'Tin, strip him of his identity, and put him in a reeducation camp. What do these camps teach? How might the North Vietnamese be more interested in someone like Y'Tin than in Tomas or Y'Juen? Discuss how these camps are really about revenge.

11. Y'Tin's father is a wise man and recognizes that different situations require different types of leaders. Describe Y'Tin as a leader. Why is he more qualified to lead in the jungle than Tomas or Y'Juen?

12. Y'Tin speaks a lot about fate, spirits, sacrifices, etc. How does this reflect the religion of his people? Explain the role of the village shaman. Y'Tin struggles to deal with the sudden anger and hatred that has filled his heart after the North Vietnamese bomb his village. Why does he think that lying on Lady's back will cleanse his heart? How are their spirits connected?

SUMMER'S YEAR HAS BEEN FILLED WITH LOTS OF THINGS, but luck sure hasn't been one of them. So it's no surprise when things go from bad to worse. But if she can't find a way to swing her family's fortune around, they could lose everything—from their jobs as migrant workers to the very house they live in. Desperate to help, Summer takes action. After all, there's just no way things can get any *worse* . . . right?

By CYNTHIA KADOHATA, the Newbery Medal-winning author of KIRA-KIRA

atheneum   From Atheneum Books for Young Readers | KIDS.SimonandSchuster.com

what if no one could hear you?
would they think you had nothing to say?

Melody has a photographic memory. She remembers every word that is spoken around her and every fact she has ever learned. Melody also has cerebral palsy, and is entirely unable to communicate. It's enough to make a girl go out of her mind.

 Then she discovers a computerized talking device that will allow her to communicate for the first time ever. It's a dream come true! But what if her teachers, her classmates, her friends don't want to hear what Melody has to say? What will become of her dreams? What will become of her life?

From award-winning author **Sharon M. Draper** comes a book as heartbreaking as it is hopeful, about a girl you'll never forget.

From Atheneum Books for Young Readers
Published by Simon & Schuster
KIDS.SimonandSchuster.com

EBOOK EDITION ALSO AVAILABLE

Meet Bingo and J'miah. They are going to save their beloved Sugar Man Swamp from a gator wrestler determined to turn it into an alligator-and-pony show and from a herd of feral hogs, and they are going to discover art on the way. For they are Scouts. They are best brothers. They are raccoons on a mission!

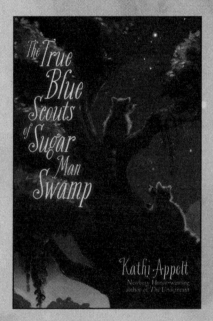

From Kathi Appelt, author of the Newbery Honor Book and National Book Award finalist THE UNDERNEATH.

Leon Leyson was only ten years old whe:
Nazis invaded Poland and his life changed fo

THE
BOY ON
THE WOODEN BOX

*How the impossible
became possible…
on Schindler's list*

A MEMOIR
LEON LEYSON
with MARILYN J. HARRAN & ELISABETH B. LEYSON

*A legacy of hope from one of the youngest children
on Schindler's list to survive*

atheneum